EVERYONE IS DRAWN to Stam Hamilton, bright, impulsive, dreamer Stam. And no one more than his younger brother Chance—a sensible, realistic kid—who is certain that Stam will find a very special place in the world someday, a place they both will share.

Now, in the lazy Colorado summer, his college days behind him, Stam's search begins—but not at all the way Chance had imagined it! First there's Stam's being in to a bookie for a thousand dollars and joking about it. Then there's his kid brother, worried sick that Stam will end up at the bottom of a river.

Drifting from job to job, joking his way in and out of trouble, taking responsibility for nothing, Stam is happily going nowhere fast—while Chance does all his worrying.

Chance's resourceful and unflagging efforts to help his brother cost him more than sleepless nights, but he keeps trying. "Because if Stam could find his way to go, his place, it would be mine too."

Or would it?

Pat Lawler has written a thoughtfully humorous, gently probing, and altogether refreshing first novel about the relationship of two brothers who must, in the end, each find his own way to grow up.

My Brother's Place

My Brother's Place

a novel by
Pat Lawler

Pantheon Books

for my mother
ALICE B. LAWLER
who told me
I could do anything

My Brother's Place

chapter 1

I'LL NEVER FORGET the day it all started—or at least it started for me. It was in June last year, early in the morning, actually just about dawn, when my brother, Stam, came into my room and woke me up.

"Hey, Chance," he said, shaking me, "how would you like to see the dew sparkling on the grass?"

I thought it was a stupid thing to say, practically in the middle of the night, so I answered, "How would you like to screw yourself?" I used to say things like that a lot last year when I was fifteen. I thought it was mature, for crissake.

"Oh, come on out," he said. "You'll really like it."

Well, he knew I would do it, and I knew I would do it. There is something about Stam that makes people usually do anything he wants. Because most of the time it is something different and pretty much fun. Stamford Hamilton—that's my brother's full name, and he was twenty-one then and just graduated from college. So now we were all expecting him to do something really great because he was so smart. But crazy too—you know, so nobody was sure what it was going to be. Everybody in our family is smart—even my sister, Del, who lives in Rome, Italy, and works for the government. That's the U.S. Government of course. Her name is really Delicia, and mine is Chance, honest to God, although a lot of teachers think it is Chauncey. My mother is the one who thought of our names, probably because she is a writer. Dad teaches elementary school and if it had been up to him, we would have been Dick and Jane and probably Spot. That's a joke. My mother and father are Lora and Charlie.

We live in the city of Lakewood, Colorado, which is a suburb of Denver, but not one of those fancy ones you read about. Most of the people in Lakewood are middle middle class and if they ever get to be upper middle, they get the hell out. We would probably be upper middle since my dad is a schoolteacher, and that is professional. But we never have enough money, and that's lower middle. So I figure out we are middle middle, like everybody else. But not in the same way as everybody else. Nothing we do or have turns out like everybody else. Sometimes when you're fifteen, you don't like it that well—being different, I mean. Sometimes what you want more than anything is just to be a plain person in a plain house doing normal things.

Last year that's what I wanted—to be like other people, but maybe richer. I thought I might like to be a Middle American. All of us wanted something last year. Dad wanted to be a principal; Mom wanted to write a book. And Stam? What did he want? It would be something different, for sure.

When Stam woke me up at dawn that June morning to see the dew on the grass, I remember I thought that he was probably the only twenty-one-year-old guy in Denver doing stuff like that. Except for poets, and I guess they do those things all the time. If it had been anybody but Stam, I would have thought he was retarded or maybe queer. But anybody who knows Stam, knows that he's not either one. He does crazy things, that's for sure; but if you're ever lucky enough to do them with him, you're glad.

Stam had all his clothes on so I knew he hadn't been to bed yet. Because if he'd just gotten up, he would have gone right out in the yard in his underwear. My dad is this way too. I've never seen anybody else's father in his underpants, but I guess everybody for miles around has seen my dad in his wild boxer shorts because he is never embarrassed by stuff like that. Most fathers wear robes if they have to walk around with their clothes off for some reason. My father doesn't even have a robe. Mom bought him one, but I think he threw it away or hid it because he never did wear it. He has an old corduroy jacket that he wears over his shorts when it is winter—so he won't get cold, I guess. But is my father crazy, or is he just his own person? Stam's the same way.

I figured Stam had been out with some girl all night, probably laying her. I would have liked to ask him, but I never would in a million years. Because he is a very private person about things like that and only tells stuff if he happens to feel like it, which isn't often.

When Stam and I went out into the yard that morning, it really was very nice. Misty and pink and soft-looking. And the dew was sparkling just the way he said. We sat for a long time without talking. Stam is a person you can do that with. Not many people are that way, especially in our family.

We sat on the sidewalk instead of the grass that morning because our lawn is really spiky. Nobody knows why, but it hurts your legs to sit on it. Well, I am sure that somebody would know why, but nobody around here does. Once in a while Mom goes out in the yard and throws her hands up in the air and says, "Migawd, I suppose we ought to mulch or aerate or something." Then she goes back in the house and works on a confession story, which is what she writes mostly, because she can sell them.

Someday I would like to have a yard like other people do. I think I would like to know about compost and spraying roses and even mulching. I know I am headed straight for the Establishment when I feel like that. I don't always—feel like that, I mean. Sometimes I think a lawn full of golden dandelions is beautiful. I really do.

But that morning with Stam, the sidewalk felt nice

and cool against my bare legs under my cutoffs, and in the dim dawn light our yard didn't look that bad.

"I wonder how much longer it is going to last," I said then. "The world, I mean. I hope it is going to last long enough for me to grow up and do my things."

"The world is four and one-half billion years old," Stam said. "Doesn't that give you a message?"

"But it's doomed," I said. "We learn that in school all the time—how it's doomed. Scientists are proving every day that we are running out of everything—food and water and fuel and even oxygen. Someday there will be only about two feet of space for everybody. We'll all just have to stand up all the time. At this rate, the world can't last much longer."

"Oh, I think it will," Stam said.

He never wants to hear anything about pollution, or oil slicks either. He thinks the world is just going to keep turning; and when he says it, somehow I think it will too. Of course it may be turning backward. I mean, you can't just completely ignore science, can you? Stam can though.

We sat quietly for a while in the nice morning world, and finally Stam sighed and said, "Well, it looks like it's time, Chance."

"Time for what?"

"Time for me to get out and go somewhere and do something. I'm twenty-one now," he said, "and I'd better get moving."

I didn't say a word; I hoped he didn't mean he was

going somewhere right away. I wanted him to wait until I was old enough to go with him.

"But what?" he said. "And where? Or even how?"

"There'll be a really good place for you, Stam," I said because I believed it.

"Sometimes I almost have it," he said, "when I'm playing my drums or reading something great. It's there right in front of me—my place, my way to go. It's there somewhere," he said. Like it was something that was lost in his room, and he hoped he'd find it any day.

"You're right at the beginning of it all," I told him, "twenty-one and a college graduate. What could be sweeter?" I asked. Because when you're fifteen, twenty-one seems like the greatest age there is.

"An English major," he said. "I'm an English major. And I'm not even sure why, except I like Shakespeare. But liking Shakespeare can't be a life's work."

"Oh, I don't know," I said. "You could be a Shakespearean scholar, I guess."

"But where do you apply?" he asked. "And would somebody actually pay you? Annotating and defining and delineating—I'd have to get a doctorate to do that."

"So maybe you can," I said. "Maybe you can get a doctorate."

"I doubt if I'm going to live long enough," he said.

"You look okay to me," I said. He looks fine. My brother is big and strong and sort of a golden color, even his hair.

"I look okay now," he said, "but after all my bones

are broken and I am dumped in the Platte River in a sack of cement, I may not look too good."

Always kidding. I knew that he was kidding. "Why?" I pointed out reasonably. "Why would you be?"

"Because I have to give somebody one thousand dollars," he said, "and I don't have one thousand dollars. I don't see how I ever will either."

If this was one of his jokes, I didn't think it was that funny. And I didn't like the look on his face, the serious look on his face. "The underworld, no doubt," I said, trying to make it a joke.

"I think so, Chance," he said. "I really think so."

"What in the hell are you talking about?" I asked him. "I wish you'd just say what you're talking about."

"I wasn't going to mention it," he said, "because it's such a nice day and it doesn't do any good anyway, talking about it. But I do think about it a lot." He shook his head like he'd rather not think about it at all.

"Well—" I said. "Well?"

"I owe a bookie a thousand dollars," he said then.

"A bookie? A bookie! Jesus H. Christ," I said.

"Yeah," Stam said. "It is sort of sickening, isn't it?" It was sickening all right.

"It was last week," he said, "and Cincy was favored over the Giants five to two. I've always liked the Giants. Needless to say, I don't like them that much anymore. So anyhow I thought I could win twenty-five hundred dollars and go around the world and find my place and not have to worry about anything for awhile. I bet one thousand dollars because it was five to two. I was a little bit drunk when I did it," he added.

"But how could you if you didn't have it?" I asked him. "How could you bet one thousand dollars you didn't have? Didn't anybody notice that you didn't have it? A thing like that, you'd think somebody would notice."

"Oh, it was over the phone," Stam said. "That stuff is always over the phone. This guy I know knows this other guy who bartends at this certain bar and he is the one who knows the bookie. It was all sort of a mistake," Stam said, "and they really shouldn't have let me do it."

"Well, if it was over the phone and—you didn't tell him your name, did you?"

"Sure I told him my name," Stam said. "How could I get the money if I didn't tell him my name?"

"Maybe he won't be able to find you," I said, "since our name isn't in the phone book." We have an unlisted phone because of my dad being a schoolteacher and little kids calling him up all the time to ask if there's going to be school when it snows or asking him if they have to do their geography since their aunt came, stuff like that.

"But this bartender knows this other guy, and he knows me," said Stam.

"Who's the guy who knows you?" I asked him.

"Jerry," said Stam and looked uneasy.

As well he might—as well he should. Because Jerry

is the original bad-luck kid. He's just as good a guy as you'll find, but it seems like some witch or something put a curse on him when he was born and things happen to him all the time. He loses things and breaks them—people steal his car. When he was in college, dogs ate his term papers or cats wet on them. You get the picture.

"Jerry," I echoed. "Well, he won't tell them where to find you. You know Jerry would never tell, Stam, no matter what they did to him."

"Oh, I couldn't let something happen to Jerry because he wouldn't tell," Stam said. "I certainly couldn't do that."

"Well, both of you had better stay away from that bar," I said. "That's the only thing to do."

"Oh, right. Absolutely. That's what we're going to do for openers," Stam said. "Just what we're going to do for closers, I don't know."

"Have you told Mom and Dad?" I asked him.

"Surely you jest," Stam said in that college way he talks. "I certainly haven't told them, and don't you tell them either, Chance. You know Mom would have a fit."

Yes, she would—my mom would have a fit. She really likes all her children quite a lot and if she thought somebody might be going to kill one of them, who knew what she might do. She might go right over to that bar and start hitting people. Which wouldn't do any good.

"Oh, well," Stam said now, "something might turn up. What do you say we play a little ball, Chance? It is a really great day and we may as well like it as much as we can."

"Okay." I didn't really feel like playing ball. I didn't even know if I'd be able to play ball ever again—or do anything. Why did this have to happen anyway, just when my favorite part of the year was starting? What were we going to do? I was glad he had told me though. I was his brother, and I would try to help him.

So we went into the house to get our gloves and a ball. I found mine right away and then went to Stam's room to help him look for his. Mom always said that if anyone from the Health Department saw Stam's room, they'd probably condemn the whole house. It really was kind of sickening because there were glasses with milk dried on them, chicken bones, and a peanut butter sandwich on the desk that looked like it ought to be buried. But he had two walls of book shelves and his drums right in the middle of the room and a great tape player. There were tapes all over and some college term papers, and I knew he kept his stack of girlie magazines under the bed because I got them out and looked at them when he wasn't home. I couldn't believe the great big boobs on those girls. If there was anything like that at my school, it would cause a riot. Anyhow, we finally found his glove under the bass drum, and we went on outside to hit a few.

There is a big vacant lot across the street behind our house, and that is where we always play ball. Stam

and I have played ball there a lot, but I will always
remember that day. Partly because of the thousand
dollars but also because we had a very good time. How
could we? With a thousand-dollar worry, how could
we? I don't know, I only know that we did. For one
thing, it was one of Colorado's best kind of days, with
a bright blue sky and little piles of clouds that moved
from place to place like sheep that were grazing there.
The mountains seemed close that day and blue and
green; and the highest one still had snow on the top.
I remember it all, how it looked and how I felt—worried
but happy too because my brother and I were playing
ball together. I can even see Stam's big, wide grin when
he hit a line drive that went over the fence and into
the tall grasses that covered the field.

It was the only ball we had with us so we both
climbed over the fence and tramped up and down looking for it. The grass was almost as high as our waists,
and it was just like looking for a needle in a haystack,
as Grandmother Hamilton always says. But it was fun
walking up and down and smelling the juice of that tall
grass where we tramped on it. We walked clear down to
the far end and stood looking back at the field covered
with that pale green grass.

"We've never seen the ocean, Chance," Stam said,
and I knew what he meant.

"You'll get to see the ocean," I told him because I
thought maybe he was thinking about the money again

and wondering if he was going to live long enough to ever see anything. I didn't want to think about that, and I didn't want him to think about it either.

Stam pulled a couple of pieces of grass, and we walked along chewing them. "One time I thought of being a sailor," he said.

I remembered that time when he was eighteen. He was going to enlist in the navy, but Mom didn't get him up in the morning and by the time he woke up himself, he decided to play golf instead.

I guess he and I both were thinking that maybe being a sailor would be better than being an English major who owed a bookie. I wished that I could help him. I wished that I could make it all right for him. For some reason, a lot of the time I feel like I'm the one who is older instead of Stam. Don't ask me why—sometimes it seems like he's the little brother.

Then I did something pretty crazy, but I've done it before and it always turns out. "Hey, Stam," I said, "if we can find the ball, it will mean that everything is going to turn out okay—the money, your place, every-thing."

He never said a word about Gee, that's dumb, but just turned around and started going down the field again looking for the ball. We must have been there about an hour tramping up and down that field, walking side by side and scuffing through the tall grass. I began to wish that I hadn't said it because now if we didn't find it, it would be bad luck. And that was really dumb of course, because finding a ball didn't really mean that much. It wasn't as if it was solid gold or would tell your fortune like those crystal ones. But what I'd said had made it important. You can do that with lots of things— it's really scary. You can make something good or bad luck just by what you say about it.

So when I said that finding the ball would be a lucky sign for Stam, I was fooling around with stuff I didn't even understand. But when we'd just about covered the field, and I thought that ball was lost for sure, I found it. It had rolled into a hole under the grass, and I walked on it. I almost fell down when I stumbled on that ball, but I knew what it was right away.

"Here." I picked it up and handed it to Stam. I thought maybe he'd forgotten what I said, but the way he held it on his palm and stared at it, I knew that he hadn't.

"Will it matter, Chance," he asked finally, "that I didn't find it myself?"

"No, it won't matter," I told him, and I didn't think that it would, "because I'm your brother."

"I'd like a chocolate malt," Stam said then, "wouldn't you?"

"Your money," I said. After all, a dollar wasn't going to make much difference, was it?

chapter 2

WHEN WE GOT BACK from the drive-in, Mom was sitting at the kitchen table typing. She had black smudges on her nose so I knew she must have put a new ribbon in her typewriter. Usually I do it for her, and I guessed she'd been pretty mad she couldn't find me. She had on my red bandanna headband that I wear for tennis, and she had it on wrong, naturally. All her hair was pushed on top of her head so it looked like a pile of dark feathers. Actually, it didn't look bad like that.

"Migawd," she said as soon as Stam and I came in, "what do you guys know about love slaves?"

"I'd like to have one," Stam said.

"What do you want to know, Mom?" I asked her, not that I'm exactly an expert on love slaves.

"Well, would a love slave draw the line at being a sacrifice for a satanic ritual?"

"Love slaves don't draw too many lines," I said, "but I think that might be one of them."

"Oh, hell," Mom said. "It is absolutely essential that this stupid girl agree to the sacrifice bit so this patrolman she always hated and called pig could save her."

"What if she's hypnotized?" I asked my mom. "She could be hypnotized."

I am used to that kind of stuff from my mother. Whenever I come into the house, she hardly ever says hello to me or how was school or whatever. She just starts sounding off about some confession story she's writing. I don't mind that much though, because at least my mother is not boring. Most of the guys I know have pretty boring mothers. They always ask you the same stuff. You could just carry around a page already written out with the answers—pretty good, not bad, feeling better—and just point to the right answer. Actually, most of the questions have the same answer—Okay, I guess.

I'll tell you the kind of stuff my mother says to my friends. She asked Skeeters Bennet if he had any ideas about Biafra. Hell, Skeeters doesn't have any ideas about anything. He can hardly even get up in the morning and tie his own shoes. She pointed her finger at John McKay and told him that the future of the country was up to him and his ilk. That's what she said—"your ilk." John probably even thought that "ilk" was a dirty word. But she's not boring.

"Hypnotized," Mom said now. "Hey, that's not bad, Chance. That's not bad at all." She started typing again but stopped after a couple of lines and said, "Don't forget Uncle Al's tonight."

"Tonight?" asked Stam. "Uncle Al's?"

It was Uncle Al's birthday, I remembered, and Aunt Willa was having us over for cake and ice cream. Willa is my mother's sister, but they're not very much alike. For one thing, Al is rich, so that makes Willa slim. At least that's what my mother says. "Because she eats something besides spaghetti," Mom says. I think this makes Dad feel bad because he is only a schoolteacher and not as good a provider as Uncle Al. But I don't know—Aunt Willa doesn't seem to have that good a time. Oh, she has all kinds of clothes and a lot of wigs of different colors. But they look just like wigs sitting on top of her head; and she has this sad look on her face most of the time. Whether it is on account of the wigs or on account of Uncle Al, I don't know. Because Al owns a lot of things, and Willa is one of them and a subsidiary at that, you can tell. Before she says anything at all, she looks at Al to see if it's all right, and usually it isn't. I doubt if Al has ever heard of women's liberation, and I wouldn't want to be the one to tell him about it. My mother says she would kill Al if she was married to him. But I don't know, I think he would just have her liquidated or amortized or something. I have heard that Al had a very poor childhood and sold shoe strings or something when he was only four years old, but I

don't believe it. I don't think he ever was four years old
or even born for that matter. I think somebody just
carved Al out of granite. But this was supposed to be
his birthday, so I could be wrong.

Uncle Al is the only rich person we know, and so I
wondered if I could get the thousand dollars for Stam
from him. He could give it to me all right if he wanted
to, but I knew he wouldn't want to. Especially if he
knew what it was for. Al would think making a bet on
a baseball game was a pretty stupid thing to do. I sort
of thought so myself, but I didn't just consider it a crime
against nature, which I thought Al probably would. So
I couldn't tell him the truth. What could I tell Al to
persuade him to give me one thousand dollars? I
thought about it all afternoon, and finally I came up
with a plan. Now all I had to do was get him alone and
put it to him.

Which wasn't easy. Al just sat in his big chair, not
even smiling on his birthday. He kept looking around
like he was wasting money just by being there, since
none of us were worth merging with. Sonia and Letty
were there too, Al and Willa's daughters, and what a
pair. Sonia is a Jesus freak and pretty ugly with teeth
that stick out farther than her chest. Letty is the older
one, nineteen to be exact, and there's nothing wrong
with her chest or the rest of her either. She is always
trying to get Stam to go out with her or down into the
basement or even into the closet with her, but he says
that fooling around with a nympho is just like eating

Chinese food. I don't know what that's supposed to mean.

After we had the cake, Al took Dad out in the back yard to bend some iron bars. There is one thing that Al really likes to do, one thing that brings the sparkle to his eyes, and that is bending iron bars. He keeps a whole pile of them in his back yard just so he can bend them. He had a big floodlight in the yard so it was plenty light, and he would pick up a bar and bend it and then hand it to Dad. Dad just stared and put it down kind of casually. Maybe you can put one bar down casually while you're talking, but after the sixth one, it gets kind of noticeable.

Finally Dad said, "Listen, Al, I'm a schoolteacher, not a muscle man, for crissake."

That always makes Al mad when somebody mentions that Dad is a teacher. Because Al didn't go to college or even high school probably. I think he had his own brickyard when he was sixteen, and he doesn't like it when other people have education.

"A schoolteacher," he said to my dad then, "listen Charlie, I could find a place for you somewhere, a real job. Anytime you get tired of that schoolteacher crap, you come to me."

Dad looked ashamed of himself, standing next to that rich man who could bend iron bars.

"You could do more for Lora and the kids," Al said, "if you had some real money."

I really hated that sonofabitch Al for making Dad feel like a failure. If he could only get to be a principal! How many years had he been waiting and hoping? But every year when the promotion lists came out, Dad wasn't on them. Every year Dad was just a teacher, which we didn't mind but he did.

"We get along okay," I said to my Uncle Al now. "Maybe Dad could help you sometime," I said to him like I'd just thought of it, "if you have to make a speech or write a letter or want to know about grammar or the right words to use."

My dad looked kind of surprised, and Al looked furious. I thought for a minute maybe he'd just pick me up and bend me double. But he snorted out laughing.

"Come around when you get a little older, Chance," he said to me. "Maybe you and I can talk business someday."

"I'm going to be a teacher," I said, "like Dad."

Al was still grinning at me. I never saw him so jolly before. "Not you, kid," he said.

It made me mad and confused too. Because what if he could see it in me, that I was going to turn out to be a cold sonofabitch like him instead of a nice guy like my dad? The confusing part of it was that while I was mad, I was proud too. And I thought maybe I really could get the thousand dollars from Al if I could just get him alone.

What I did was wait till he went to the bathroom. Oh,

I didn't go in with him, at least not until he got through. Asking somebody for money when he's taking a leak doesn't seem like very good business.

So, as I say, I waited until Al was coming out the bathroom door and there I was, and I kind of edged him back in.

"Can I talk to you for a minute, Uncle Al?" I asked him and I sat down on the edge of the bathtub and waved a hand at the toilet just like it was a conference chair.

Well, he didn't really want to sit down on the toilet and talk to me, you could tell that; but he did.

"You know I have a paper route," I said first, and he nodded although I doubted if he'd ever thought about it before. "I have figured out how I can double my profits," I said.

He smiled at that. Double profits are the sweetest words in the world to a businessman. But what do you want from me? I could see that he was thinking that, so I let him have it.

"If you will loan me one thousand dollars," I said to Al, "I can buy a motorbike and handle a route twice as big as the one I've got." I said it all real fast before I could get nervous about it. Because of course the kicker was—how could I pay him back? Because I couldn't actually buy a motorbike or how would I have the money for Stam? And if I didn't, I couldn't get a bigger route and how would I ever pay Al back? But I decided I'd worry about that later. Maybe I could give him fifty cents a week for all eternity. One thing for sure: it would be better for me to owe Uncle Al than for Stam to owe a bookie.

"Well, well," said Al, "so I was right about you. You really do have a head on your shoulders."

Was he going to do it? It sounded like maybe he would do it.

"I might consider that, Chance," he said, "but there are some parts that need fleshing out. For instance, interest. What had you thought of for interest?"

Interest? I hadn't even thought of interest. Maybe eternity wouldn't be long enough for me to pay him back.

"What do you think?" I stammered.

"Since you're in the family, two percent," he said kindly. "And of course I'll have to hold the title to the bike until you get the loan paid off. It's only business, Chance," he said with what he probably thought was a kindly smile. "I wouldn't be doing you a favor if I gave you the idea that you can get something for nothing. Not in this old world, boy."

Not even if your brother might get killed or his bones broken? That wouldn't be something for nothing —that would be something for something. Maybe Al would have given it to me if I'd told him the truth and begged him, but it seemed like I'd be letting Dad down if I did that. I had to think of Dad too.

"And of course," Al said, "we'd have to tell your dad about this. I couldn't loan you money without telling

Charlie since you are not legally of age nor responsible for your own debts."

So that did it. I couldn't give him the title to a motorbike I didn't intend to buy and if he was going to tell Dad anyway, what was the use?

"I like your thinking, Chance," Al said. "You've got your head screwed on right for sure."

So I had a head on my shoulders and it was screwed on right, but I still didn't have any money, so what good did it do? "I don't think Dad would like it," I said to Al. "Dad doesn't like us borrowing money."

"He sure is a proud bastard, isn't he?" Al shook his head like Dad was just beyond him. Al got off the toilet then and opened the door into the hall. "I meant what I said about coming around when you're older, kid. You and I can do some business someday."

Never. I still wanted to be rich someday, but I hoped I'd never be like Al—asking his own nephew for interest! If my dad had one thousand dollars, he would just give it to anyone who needed it. And that's probably why he doesn't have it and Al does.

After Al and I had our talk, I felt so bad I just went out in the back yard alone. I had hoped so much I could get the money from him. He was the only one I knew who could have given it to me. What was I going to do now? What was Stam going to do?

It was dark in the yard since Al had turned the light off after he got through bending iron bars, but I was glad it was dark. Sometimes you feel like being in the dark all by yourself, and this was one of those times.

But when I went by the shed in the patio, somebody whispered, "Chance, come here." I knew right away it was Sonia. Like I said before, or maybe I didn't, I don't really like Sonia, but I was curious about what she was doing in the shed so I went in.

She was sitting on a blanket, and I could see by the light that shone out the kitchen door that she was looking cross-eyed. "Sit down, Chance," she said, patting the blanket, "by me."

I got a whiff of her breath then and I knew that old Sonia was not only cross-eyed, she was pie-eyed. You know—drunk. That Jesus freak was honest-to-God drunk. I don't even like her when she's sober, and I sure didn't want to have anything to do with her when she was drunk.

"I've got to be going, Sonia," I said.

She grabbed one of my hands then and put it down the neck of her dress. "Do you want to have some fun, Chance?" she said, breathing hard, and then she hiccoughed.

Well, here I was with a real chance to lose my virginity, which I never had done yet, and I was fifteen, and all I really wanted to do was to get the hell out of there.

I pulled my hand off her breast, and she didn't have them like her sister, Letty, or maybe I wouldn't have. But she grabbed my hand again. It made me feel terrible, I'll tell you, like something was wrong with me, like maybe I was homo or something. Because the guys at school said it didn't matter if the girl was good-looking or you liked her or anything like that. And here it turned out I was the kind of a guy who couldn't do it if I didn't like the girl. And maybe I couldn't even then—who knew? Maybe I'd grow up and get married and go on my honeymoon and then—nothing. Boy, I sure wished I'd never gone into the shed.

"I thought Jesus people didn't drink," I said to Sonia then, trying to get her mind off sex.

Well, godalmighty, if she didn't start to cry, and her nose started running and she looked about ten times worse than she had before. "I'm a human being too," she snuffled, "just like Letty. I need love too."

Yeah, I thought, that was probably true. Here was ugly, flat-chested Sonia with a sister like Letty and no wonder she was neurotic. Probably she did need love. But I just couldn't manage to give it to her.

I didn't know what to do or say or how to get out of it. Finally I said, "Jesus loves you." It reminded me of the old song I used to sing in Sunday school when I was a little kid and I could hardly keep myself from singing the rest of it, "this I know, for the Bible tells me so." Lots of times I feel like doing crazy things like that and sometimes I do, but this time I didn't because I knew it would really tick Sonia off and maybe she'd just rape me or something. Of course she couldn't actually rape me. Women can't do that to men because it's physically impossible. But I didn't want her even trying.

Then Sonia said something really wicked. "Jesus can't screw me," is what she said. It scared me, it really did. I had the feeling that a bolt from heaven might strike us both dead.

I got up off that blanket fast and pulled old Sonia up with me. I kind of tugged the neck of her dress together where she'd pulled it apart to show me her skimpy little tits. "Come on in the house and get some coffee," I said, "and then you'll feel better. You're just lucky, Sonia, that I'm not the kind of a guy to take advantage of you when you don't know what you're doing. You'll thank me tomorrow."

I opened the shed door and looked around pretty carefully to be sure nobody saw me coming out of there with her. I never would have lived it down if anybody had.

She didn't want to go. She kept whimpering and snuffling. "Come on, Chance—I really want to do it. Your mother will never know, Chance."

That was just about the worst thing she could have said—about my mother. It made me sound like a baby, and right then I just hated Sonia and I jerked her and said, "Shut up!"

I took her into the kitchen, and thank God nobody was there, and I poured her some coffee and set her down sort of behind the door. I made her drink the coffee too and then took her outdoors again and walked her around the block. I would have left her flat, but I was afraid she might go into the living room where everybody was and just blurt out the whole thing. She was drunk enough, believe me. And I would have had to commit suicide or run away from home.

It took me about an hour to sober old Sonia up and once, when we were on our fifth time around the block, she stopped all of a sudden and threw up. On my shoes. I never have hated anybody as much as I hated Sonia. I was afraid the experience would turn me off sex for my whole life.

But after she got sick, Sonia got sober too. And when she did, she naturally blamed me for the whole thing. She even acted like I was the one who got her drunk in the first place. "You're evil, Chance Hamilton," she said, "and I never want to see you again."

"Mutual," I said, and I couldn't help adding, "you stupid bitch."

She snorted so hard I was afraid she was going to throw up again. "After what you tried to do—"

"Now wait a minute," I said. I wasn't going to let her get away with that. And then I thought—oh, what the hell, why not? Why not let her think that or at least say it if it made her feel better? She sure wasn't going to spread it around because she knew that I knew how it really was. Don't ask me why I didn't make the stupid broad admit it. I just don't think anybody should have to feel more ashamed than they can stand.

So I said, "What if we act like it never happened?"

"I think that would be best," she said stiffly. So she knew all right, and I was glad I'd let her off the hook. But I don't know—I was really depressed. When somebody is supposed to be so good and even goes around calling everybody's attention to her goodness, and then it turns out it's only because she hasn't any choice, it's pretty disillusioning. I was glad when the party was over and we got to go home.

I was feeling lousy by that time—Al, Sonia, the whole evening. Stam had gone off with Letty somewhere, and I couldn't understand that either after what he'd said about her. Oh, well, maybe he just felt like Chinese food. Of course he was worried. Stam wasn't really himself, I thought, because he was so worried.

Mom went out to the kitchen as soon as we got home and said she still had our supper dishes to wash, and Dad went right along behind her and said, "Couldn't you do that tomorrow, Lora?" He patted her on the shoulder the way he does sometimes, and she ruffled his hair the way she does and smiled at him.

"I don't know why not, Charlie," she said, and pretty soon they went off to their room together. Well, I knew what that meant. More sex. For some stupid reason, it really made me sad.

That night when I got in bed, I did something I hadn't done for years. I got Mr. Bear out of the closet. He is the big stuffed bear Stam gave me when I was born. He's been lying on the closet shelf ever since I got older. But I took Mr. Bear out of the closet and put him under the covers in my bed. I made sure to cover him up good so if my mother happened to come in during the night, she wouldn't see him. I didn't think she'd be coming in though.

chapter 3

I FIGURED the summer was just going to be zilch, but it is hard to be miserable in Colorado when the sky is beaming and blue. I got up early every morning and rode my bike up to the ballpark for practice. Every summer I decide that I am going to be a major league outfielder for my career. In the winter I sometimes think I might be a business tycoon, a real Establishment, Middle American kind of a guy. My family has never really been a part of any of that. For instance, we have a house in the suburbs, but we don't have a basement. Almost all houses in the suburbs have basements. It's practically a law. If I wasn't kind of a wheel at school, I would be an outcast since we don't have a basement. Stam says that is the most idiotic kind of conformity, but I don't know. I wouldn't mind having a basement with wood paneling and all.

But last summer I didn't worry about basements. I

had enough to worry about with Stam in to a bookie for a thousand dollars. When I rode to the ballpark every morning, I would start off by being worried. But it only took me a couple of blocks before I felt better. For one thing, I was all alone, which was really nice. There is always someone at our house even if it's just the people who live there. Which it hardly ever is. I have friends over and Stam has friends over, but it is mostly Stam's friends. The guys. That's what we call them— the guys—and you would think they were all orphans the way they hang around our house and eat there and even sleep there part of the time. Doug, for instance, gets drunk quite a lot and passes out on our couch for ten to twelve hours at a time. But when Mom gets up in the morning and sees him there, she just says, "Migawd," and goes through to the kitchen. She never throws him out though.

But when I was on my bike riding to ball practice, I didn't think of Doug or Jerry or Phil or any of them. I just tasted how good the air was before the smog moved in and I liked the look of the sky and the mountains, which look so close early in the morning. And practice was neat too, playing ball without the pressure of being in a game. I was plenty tired and sweaty but feeling loose and easy by the time I headed home.

At home I always had a big glass of orange juice with ice cubes in it, and it seemed to me like I was drinking a glass of sunshine. I never said that to anybody. I would just as soon put on one of those short skirts ballet dancers wear and whirl around as say I was drinking a glass of sunshine. A lot of things you think like that, and you enjoy thinking them, but it's better if you keep them to yourself.

So after I'd had my breakfast, Stam got out of bed and had his. Then we went places, did things, and had fun. Having fun all through June and then it was July and Stam still hadn't gotten a job. I heard Mom and Dad talking about it quite a lot.

"When is Stam going to do something?" Dad asked. "Can an English major actually do anything?"

"Now, Charlie," my mother said, "one of these days Stam will find his field."

"And when he does, he'll probably lie down in it," Dad said. Which I thought was pretty funny, but Mom didn't.

"Now, listen here, Charlie Hamilton, you know Stam went through college in three years and he was on the Dean's List every semester too."

"I know," Dad said. "I know all that, Lora. But, remember, it still takes a quarter to get on the bus. Is he ever going to have a quarter to get on the bus?"

"Well," said my mother, "getting on the bus isn't everything. Sometimes just strolling down life's way is better."

How about that? Strolling sounded like something Stam would go for all right, but it would be nice if he had some quarters too. Or a thousand. Especially a thousand. Where was Stam going to get a thousand?

But Stam and I had really good times together last summer. In the afternoons we would play tennis or golf or drive up in the mountains and hike around. I would rather go hiking with Stam than anyone because he sees things that other people never even notice. He opens up those pods that fall off trees and inside there is a tiny leaf curled up and you wouldn't even know it was there if you didn't look for it. We would lie quietly on the bank of a stream and sometimes a fish would swim right up and practically stare at us. It's a funny thing, having a fish stare at you. Really surprised, you know, because you're not trying to catch it.

Sometimes Stam and I whittled sticks and then threw them in the creek to watch them float. We had races with our sticks. It was never boring with Stam, walking down a path by a creek, watching the water foam up when it hit the rocks at the rapids, seeing a bright blue-bird dart from one tree to another. Those were my favorite days last summer, those days with Stam.

But even while we were having a good time, even when everything was practically perfect, I would think about the money. What is he going to do about the money? Doesn't he care? Isn't he going to try? Is he ever going to amount to anything? He's twenty-one. When is he going to amount to something? Boy, I really hated feeling that way. Because I didn't understand it, me feeling that way.

When I was twenty-one, would I be watching fish and sleeping all day and uncurling leaves? I really liked being with my brother, doing those things with my brother, and I hated thinking those mean things about him. But I would do it, I couldn't keep from doing it. Please, Stam, I wanted to say to him, do something great pretty soon now. I had been waiting ever since I was a little kid for Stam to do something great. And maybe he wasn't going to. Maybe he wasn't ever going to. And maybe he was going to get killed before he could.

But I kept having a good time with him because everybody does have a good time with Stam. Sometimes in the afternoons he went off with his friends or I went off with mine or we all went off together. My friends and Stam's friends—we would have a ballgame with the big guys drinking beer and the little ones usually beating them because they were in better shape and not drinking beer.

When it was time for my paper route, there would be people all over the front yard, folding my papers, throwing them at each other. And Jerry always wanted to take my route—riding my bike, accidentally kicking out a spoke, throwing to the wrong houses.

"I had a paper route, you know," he said to me. "I even won prizes on my route for getting the most new customers. I won a trip to Disneyland, but I got the mumps and couldn't go. But I won it. I was a great paper boy."

I knew what a great paper boy Jerry must have been. He broke windows and dogs bit him. He lost his collection money, and people moved out without paying him. Jerry didn't have to tell me all that; I just knew.

The worst day, though, was when Jerry and Doug did my route together, Doug drunk and riding on the handlebars. He fell off twice before they even got to the corner. I couldn't stand to watch it after that. And Stam wouldn't stop them—he was laughing too hard. Besides, he wanted them to do it. There is something about Stam that just loves for people to do crazy things that they're not supposed to. And, boy, did I get the complaints from my customers after Jerry and Doug got through with my route.

"I couldn't believe my eyes," said this one old lady on the phone; "this strange-looking young man sitting on the handlebars of a bicycle threw my paper in the azalea bush. Then he got off the bicycle, fell down in the bush and just lay there for a long time." That lady doesn't know how lucky she was that Doug ever did get out of her bush, or that Jerry didn't ride right over it.

July was like that all the way through—not too bad actually. Lots of laughs—you know?

Now it was the first of August and school would be starting in another month. Stam had never said anything more to me about the money. I kept hoping he would say something, would tell me he had some kind of a plan.

One day in August he and I played tennis and then

sat down outside the court with our backs against the wire to rest.

"What are you going to do, Stam?" I asked him then. "Do you know what you're going to do yet?"

"Work on my backhand, I guess," he said. "I can't have my little brother beating me all the time."

"I mean about the money," I said. "The thousand dollars."

He looked surprised, as if he'd forgotten about the money, but I knew he couldn't have. Who could forget one thousand dollars?

"I don't know," he said. "I just don't know, Chance. I'd better get a job, for one thing. The only trouble is I don't know what kind of a job to get. What do I want to do?" he asked. "What do I want to be? What would I like to have someday?"

"You'd like to have one thousand dollars," I reminded him.

"Yeah." He sighed. "I guess I'm just going to have to get some kind of a job."

Dad always said that the only way Stam would get a job is if someone came to the house, got him out of bed, and offered him one. Well, it didn't happen quite that way. What happened was that some guy called up on the phone and asked Stam if he wanted to work at Barkeley Park.

"He said someone recommended me," Stam told Mom and me after he hung up the phone. "He said someone named Miller Hansen said I was a good worker." He shook his head. "I don't know any Miller Hansen," he said, "and even if I did, why would he say I was a good worker? I've only had about three jobs in my life."

"That gas station where you worked last summer?" I suggested.

Stam laughed. "No, I don't think it was the gas station. I didn't do a lot of things I was supposed to do there, and I did a lot of things I wasn't supposed to."

"Well, you have a job anyway," I said. "Good old Miller Hansen."

"I start tomorrow," Stam said, "and I can work for a few months until it is too cold to take care of the flowers and grass. The only reason I am getting a job in the park this late in the summer is because they lost two guys this week."

"How did they lose them?" Mom asked nervously, like she thought Barkeley Park was a jungle or something.

"One guy fell out of a tree," Stam said, "and the other one kept getting drunk and sitting in the fountain."

"You stay out of the trees, Stam," Mom said.

"How about the fountain?" Stam asked her. "Can I sit in the fountain?"

"I'll make you a big lunch," Mom said, just as if he hadn't said a word. I don't know if she treats him that way because she knows he's kidding or because she's afraid he isn't.

I was glad Stam had a job. I didn't know if he could make a thousand dollars, but at least it was a beginning. I felt so good about it that I decided to go out in the yard and tell Dad.

Dad was doing what he calls yard work. He had a pillow to sit on and a can of beer and he was pulling all the crabgrass that he could reach in a circle around him.

"Stam has a job," I told him, "at Barkeley Park. He starts tomorrow."

Dad took a swallow of beer and then he said, "Well, hallelujah. But how come he had to go to college to get a job in a park?"

"Don't knock it, Dad," I told him. "It's a job."

"Yeah," he said and tipped up the can again. Then he stood up, picked up the pillow, and followed me into the house. He is always through with his yard work as soon as his beer is gone. "At least now Stam will have to get up in the morning like the rest of the world," he said.

But Stam said he wasn't going to, at least not the first day. "I have a date tonight," he said, "so I will just stay up all night and then go to work. That way I won't have to get up in the morning. Which I hate to do," he mentioned.

And that's what he did. Along about midnight when

I was sitting up on the roof with my telescope, Stam drove up and waved at me. "Come on down, Chance," he said, "we're going on a picnic."

He had a girl with him, and Phil, who is one of the guys. They went on into the house so I climbed down off the roof and went inside too. They were in the kitchen, and Stam's girl was making sandwiches.

Stam had the refrigerator door open and was staring into it. "Sardines?" he said. "Dill pickles? Or a dish of cold pork and beans?"

"How's Sissy?" I asked Phil, not because I really wanted to know but because that's what you're supposed to say to people when they're married. Phil is the only one of the guys who is married, and he doesn't seem to enjoy it that much. Because, even though his wife is quite good-looking, she is really sickening. Phil works during the day and goes to college at night, and Sissy won't get a job or help him in any way. She buys clothes and fixes her fingernails and will hardly ever even cook anything. He says she hates sex too.

"Sissy is really mad at me," Phil said then. He has a long face and a Fu Manchu moustache that makes it look even longer. "She's pregnant," he said, "and she blames me."

"Well, you are her husband," Stam said.

"I thought that she—and she thought that I—"

"Was using contraceptives?" I suggested.

Phil looked shocked, "What do you know about contraceptives, Chance? You're only fifteen."

What didn't I know about contraceptives? Besides my Family Living class, I was personally acquainted with lots of horny guys. John McKay even carried them in his wallet all the time. "I want to be ready," he said. Well, maybe I wasn't ready or something, but I know when I was fifteen, I was the oldest virgin around; and I kept that pretty quiet, believe me. John, my best friend, had laid at least five girls; he said six but I didn't believe him because I knew that girl Sandy Miller, and I didn't think she would do it. She slapped my face once because I pushed her down in the snow and took her mittens off. It stands to reason if a girl is insulted when you take her mittens off, she's not going to let you do other stuff. Maybe it would be different though.

"Well," said Stam to Phil now, "you're going to find that you feel a lot better after you go on a picnic."

"I don't know," said Phil, "I have a feeling Sissy would be really mad about me going on a picnic when she's pregnant."

"She usually is mad at you," Stam reminded him.

"There's no way Sissy can find out about the picnic," Phil said. You could see he really wanted to go.

"Not unless you tell her," said Stam.

And that wasn't impossible because Phil tells everything. The main problem is to keep him from telling a lot of things no one wants to know. I could just picture him confessing to Sissy that he'd gone on a picnic and begging her to show compuncture. Phil uses lots of big words, and they're usually wrong.

"Where are we going on this picnic?" he asked Stam then.

"Barkeley Park," said Stam. "That's where my job starts at five a.m., and I will just stay there until time for work."

It was after one when we got there and it was really neat. Black and silver—black where the shadows were, silver in the moonlight. The fountain in the middle of the park was silver against the black.

"Listen," said Stam. "In the middle of the night, in the middle of a park, a fountain sounds different, doesn't it?"

All of us were quiet, listening. Did it sound different because we were the only ones listening? Is a sound only there when someone hears it? Kind of a whirring, tinkling, splashing sound.

We sat in a circle on the ground by the fountain eating our sandwiches and potato chips and talking. Pretty soon it began to get cold, and we got a blanket out of the car and sat on that. In Colorado, even in the summer, it gets cool at night. And if you stay out late enough, you will usually get cold. I think that's kind of a nice place to be, don't you?

It's funny the things people talk about in the middle of the night when it is quiet and dark, just things that they want to, that probably don't matter or mean a lot. Stam said that while we were sitting there, grass was growing, flowers were unfolding slowly, getting ready to bloom. He said that some places in the world, it was still yesterday.

"Just think," said Stam, "the night is filled with laughs and screams and songs, but we can't hear them. Right now somewhere people are getting on an airplane or getting off. Somebody is drinking coffee, and somebody else is meditating in a monastery."

I tried to think of all the time zones and figure out if all those things would be possible, but it was neater thinking that they were.

"Hapless girls like Sissy are getting pregnant," Stam said.

Phil spoke up then and said that Sissy wasn't getting pregnant; she was already pregnant. He sounded sort of nervous when he said that, and he added that maybe he should go home. Nobody paid any attention to him.

Belinda, Stam's girl, asked if anybody had ever noticed how sometimes strange things happen that there's no reason for? "And you can't understand no matter how you try," she said. "It was last summer that I'm thinking of, one night out at Elitch Gardens. I went dancing there with Ted, this boy from Dartmouth. Everything couldn't have been more perfect; there wasn't anything wrong with anything. I've tried to remember something, but it was just one of those really perfect dates. I had on my favorite dress, a white one with a golden belt. He had on white too—Ted had on a white suit, and he was tan and the sun had bleached his hair gold. All white and gold," Belinda said. "I could smell the flowers from the gardens while we danced, and I knew that we were a really beautiful couple. We danced together like somebody you see on the stage or in the movies. We danced every song until intermission. Then we sat down at a little table on the edge of the dance floor, and that's when the funny thing happened."

"You woke up," I said.

Belinda just gave me a look and went on talking. "He said that I was a great dancer, and I said you're pretty cool yourself. It was dark in there except for a small candle lamp in the middle of each table. But when I looked across at him, I couldn't see any light in his eyes."

"Why would there be light in his eyes," I asked, "there in the dark? Unless he was a cat or something."

"There should have been a light," Belinda said. "There should have been a reflection from the lamp, and there was nothing there."

"Maybe he was stoned," Phil said.

"No, he wasn't stoned or drunk or anything," Belinda said. "There was just nothing in his eyes. No light or anything in his eyes. I felt as if I was sitting at that table by myself. There was a body there across from me, but no one was in it."

"You were stoned," I said.

"I most certainly was not," Belinda said. "It wasn't

funny, I'll tell you. It was scary, and the strangest part of it all was that I felt so lonely."

"It had something to do with light refraction," I guessed, "and the fact that it was dark in there except for the lamps and the way they were placed."

"No, Chance," said Stam, "it had something to do with nothing and how lonely you feel when you see it."

We all looked around the circle at one another then and saw friendly eyes with moonlight in them and were glad.

All night long we talked—about dogs we'd had and were cats really smarter and did anybody know if cows were as smart as either? Things that are nice to talk about in the night. Stam drove to an all-night restaurant nearby and brought back hot coffee so he could stay awake for his job and we could stay awake with him for awhile.

It was almost dawn when we finally drove away in Phil's car with Phil promising Stam he would come back for him in the afternoon. Stam was sitting on the grass, leaning against a big tree when we left. His eyes were closed, and I hoped he wasn't going to sleep. When Stam is asleep, it is really hard to wake him up, and I didn't think his new boss would like doing that.

When we drove away, I looked back and wished that I could stay there with Stam and keep him awake. But I couldn't. Sometimes no matter how much you want to, you can't help other people. Even your brother.

chapter 4

STAM LIKED HIS JOB in the park. Of course Mom still thought he was going to turn out to be a college president or a brain surgeon, but she knew he would have to get out of bed to do either of those things, and his job in the park got him out of bed at least. Dad was really glad about Stam's job. When someone is as old as Stam, it's more normal somehow if he works. Dad wants us kids to be like everyone else. He isn't, but he wants us to be.

Mom doesn't. She says, "Dare and do." Once she said to me, "Did you ever think, Chance, that maybe there really is a Shangri-La? Somewhere in the Himalayas— it might be there. And you can go and look for it when you're grown up. Wouldn't that be great? Or dive for pearls in the Black Sea." Mom doesn't know anything about geography plus I'd have to be about fifty before she'd think I was grown up enough to do either of those things.

I guess the word for Mom is contradictory, because she wants us all to do fantastic things and yet she wants us to be perfectly safe while we're doing them. No way. You have to decide, I guess, whether to opt for a pension plan with benefits including the best hospital coverage or be on the deck of a tramp steamer in Cathay. I don't know. If you're wandering around the bazaars of India, you probably don't have a patio with a retaining wall with geraniums planted on it. And white wrought-iron furniture with a striped umbrella over it. Of course it is possible if you're rich enough. If you're rich enough, you can wander all over and have someone else repotting your geraniums or moving your lawn furniture into the shed in the winter. But it wouldn't be quite the same, would it?

I always thought that maybe someday Stam and I would go look for Shangri-La or at least check out Pigalle in Paris. When we got home again, I could start in on the geraniums and sign up for a station wagon. I have always figured that maybe there is some way to get the best of two worlds.

I liked Stam's job too. After baseball practice, I rode my bike over to Barkeley Park, and he and I ate lunch together. There was this one big bush with white flowers on it that we sat under to eat our lunch. Shady and cool and sweet-smelling with the leaves over our heads like a roof. There was a squirrel we fed every day, and Stam said he had gotten to know this squirrel pretty well since he'd been there.

"He's just like a person," Stam said. "He's a bachelor, I can tell. There is nothing of the old family man about this squirrel. For one thing, he climbs the highest branches in the trees and leaps the farthest of any squirrel I've ever seen." Stam grinned, and you could see he admired this squirrel. "I call him Gus for no particular reason," he said, "and he comes when I call him if he feels like it. Gus only does things if he feels like it. You know, Chance, I really like this job. Once a day my boss comes and yells at me to dig or water or weed. Then he goes away and I have the whole park to myself since I'm the only one working here."

"How come he yells at you?" I asked Stam. "It looks to me like you're doing a good job." Everything was green and growing—even the circular walk around the fountain was swept clean.

"He yells at me because I've been to college and have long hair," Stam said. "Also he wants me to trim everything, and I don't. He wants the flowers in straight rows; he wants the shrubs to be straight across the top. It's nicer like this. This is the way it was supposed to be."

It was beautiful in Stam's park with the flowers growing in great wild bunches and the bushes trailing green across the paths.

Stam's park—I met Tina there and fell in love with her the moment I saw her. The first time I was ever in love—Tina Morelli.

I had come to eat lunch with Stam and I had to wait

until he got through mowing so I was just walking around looking at the flowers. I picked a big dark red one from a bush although you're not supposed to do that. I knew Stam wouldn't care; every night when he came home from work, he brought Mom some of the flowers. I came down a little hill from the fountain into a kind of glade, and there was Tina. She was lying on a blanket on her stomach sunning herself in a pair of quite small shorts and a halter. Her hair was long and black, but she had it in braids, so her bare brown back could get browner, I guess. I couldn't see her face because she was lying on it, but from her legs alone I could tell that she was the most fabulous girl I had ever seen. She had a very nice back end too, I couldn't help noticing.

I just stood there staring down at her for a minute, and she turned over quickly and looked up at me. Her face was even better than her legs, but she looked scared to death with her big dark eyes wide. I guess I looked like some kind of a sex maniac staring at her that way. I may even have been breathing hard too, for all I know.

"Hi," I said. "I brought you this," and I handed her the flower. Wasn't that crazy?

But she took it from me without screaming and sat up and stuck the flower in one of her dark braids. It looked even better there than it had on the bush.

"I'm Chance Hamilton," I said then, "and this is my brother's park. I mean he works here." She still didn't say a word, just kept staring at me with those big dark eyes. "I was just walking around," I said, "and I saw you and I—" Fell in love with your legs and your ass? I couldn't very well say a thing like that so I stammered, "—and—well, I thought maybe we could talk."

She smiled then and it was like all the birds started singing and all the flowers started blooming. Isn't that corny? But that's the way it was the first time Tina smiled at me.

"Tina Morelli," she said. "Would you like to sit on my blanket?"

Would I like to sit on her blanket? Would I like to spend the rest of my life just looking at her? "Yes," I said simply and sat down.

"I really like this park," Tina said. "It is a lovely, wild place not like any other park I have ever seen."

"That's because my brother is the one who takes care of it," I told her. "He thinks this is just the way a park should be."

"Oh, it is," she said.

"Where do you go to school?" both of us said at once then and burst out laughing. It was a good sign. A lot of girls never laugh with you. Oh, sometimes at you but not that often with you. There are lots of good-looking girls at my school, but when you start talking to them, their faces just close up and they say only phony things, things that you know they think are cute.

This girl was just like a plain person instead of a girl. She said that she was a senior at South Denver High, and I said that I was a senior at Alameda in Lakewood. Actually, I was going to be a sophomore and it was going to be my first year in high school, but I couldn't tell her that, could I? I really hated to start off lying to her like that, but I practically had no choice. If I had told her I was only a little kid, she wouldn't have wasted five minutes on me. Well, maybe five as she seemed like a nice, kind girl, but she sure wouldn't have been my girl, which I wanted her to be.

Tina said that her mother and father were divorced and her mother worked as a cocktail waitress at the Tiffin, which is a classy Denver restaurant. Wasn't that sad? About her folks being divorced, I mean. Lots of kids at my school have folks that have split, and maybe even are married to somebody else, so the kids have maybe two mothers or fathers or both. I am thankful that my parents seem to think quite a lot of each other even though they fight about things like my dad leaving his fly open around the house or my mom typing all night instead of watching Lawrence Welk. But Tina didn't seem to mind that much about her folks. She didn't have tears in her eyes when she told me, for instance.

I had decided that I was going to ask her to eat lunch with Stam and me under the big white bush and even give her one of my sandwiches and some potato chips when all of a sudden, these two guys came walking up.

I got a funny, scared feeling as soon as I saw them because they didn't look like they belonged in that park. They had short hair and suits for one thing. For another, they both looked very serious and—well, menacing is the word I thought of.

And when one of them said, "We're looking for a fellow named Stam Hamilton," I just knew. Those two guys were from that bookie or maybe one of them actually was the bookie, and they were after Stam!

"He isn't here," I blurted out and just hoped that Tina wouldn't say anything as I had told her my brother was working on the other side of the park. But she didn't say a word.

"Oh?" said this one fellow who was built like a prizefighter. "We were told he works here."

"Not here," I said quickly. "He works in another park."

"Where?" said the other guy. He had a little moustache, which would have made him look funny if he hadn't looked so mean. "What park? What's the name of it?"

"I don't know," I said and stood up. When you're talking to gangsters, it's better to be on your feet. "I don't know the name of it." I didn't want them looking around the park for Stam. "I know where it is though," I told them. "I could go with you and show you where it is." Stam had two more hours to work, and I figured I could keep them away until he had a chance to get home. I hoped they didn't know where he lived too.

"Maybe we should look around here a little first," the bigger guy said.

"But he isn't here," I said, "and it's almost time for him to get off work. You'd better hurry," I said, "or you'll miss him."

"Who are you anyway?" said the moustache. "How come you know so much about him?"

"I'm his brother," I said, "and actually I was just going over to his park to ride home with him. It is quite a ways from here," I babbled, "and I was going to ride my bike over there, but I could go with you instead to help you."

"His brother, huh?" said the big guy. So now maybe they would kidnap me and hold me until Stam gave them the thousand dollars. I was scared, but I didn't know what else to do.

"Come on," I said, "let's go." Because I didn't want them to get any ideas about Tina and maybe kidnap her too.

"Well, okay," said the big guy, "if you're sure you know where it is."

"Well, actually it's City Park," I told them, having decided City Park was the biggest one, and I could stall them that much longer. Because they wouldn't do anything to me until they found Stam, I figured.

"How come you didn't remember that it was City Park?" one of them asked. "How could you forget City Park?"

"Well, I was kind of surprised," I said. "When I am surprised, my brain works slower. I have just this little bit of brain damage, you see, and when I am excited, one side of my brain doesn't work." I hated saying that in front of Tina. I figured she'd never want to have anything to do with me if she thought I was crazy. "Oh, I'm really okay," I said. "I happen to get very good grades in school and all—straight *A*'s usually but—"

"Listen kid," said the guy with the moustache, "will you can it? Just can it, please? If you know where Stam Hamilton is, come on."

"What was it you wanted with him?" I asked them. "Maybe it would be something I could tell him and save you the time."

"Business," said the big one shortly, and it seemed like my blood froze. I knew what kind of business all right.

"Well, so long," I said to Tina casually although I felt like my heart was breaking because I didn't know how I was ever going to find her again. She might not even be in the telephone book, her folks being divorced. And how would I know which Morelli if she was? It's a bad feeling having your heart aching at the same time you're scared to death. "Remember that guy I told you about?" I said to her. "He'll tell you where to reach me." I hoped she'd know I meant Stam and go look for him and tell him about these two guys. I hoped she was as smart as she looked. I also hoped that these two gorillas were as dumb as they looked.

"You can count on me," she said.

So I knew that she had gotten the message, and I

would have been happy if I wasn't so miserable. As it was, I thought that maybe I had a chance. Where there's life, there's hope, my mother always says. And I was still alive, wasn't I?

It took us about twenty minutes to get to City Park as it is in the east part of Denver and Barkeley is in the far west, which is Lakewood.

"Okay, now where?" asked the big one as we drove through the gates into the park and down the road past the lake.

"Just drive around," I said. "He should be feeding the ducks about now."

So we drove around the lake a couple of times, and the second trip around, the moustache guy said, "What does this Hamilton look like anyway? It might help if we knew what to look for."

"He has bright red hair and is six feet four and weighs around two-fifty. You can't miss him," I said, "because he is so big and tough-looking." I thought maybe that would scare them, but it didn't seem to. "I guess he's not feeding the ducks," I said. "He must be out on the island." This is an island where the monkeys stay out in the middle of the biggest lake.

"Are you sure this is the right park?" the big guy said, looking at me suspiciously like he'd just as soon drill me as not. "They told us Barkeley Park."

"I'm his brother," I said. "I ought to know, hadn't I? What we'd better do," I said, "is get a rowboat and go out to the island." Once we got out there, I decided, I would think of some way to keep them there until I figured Stam had had time to get home.

"Why don't we just wait for him to come in?" said one of the guys. "I don't like rowboats; I can't swim." So maybe I could drown him if I had to. I hoped I wouldn't have to. I didn't want to actually kill anyone if I could avoid it.

"We can't wait for him to come in," I said, "if we're not sure he's there. I think he must be, but he might not be."

"Hell!" said the big guy. "So let's get a rowboat."

What they do at City Park is rent rowboats for people to get out on the lake, so we rented one, and I had to row since neither of those guys knew how. I took as long as I could getting to the island, even going around in circles a couple of times until one of them noticed.

"What's the matter with you, kid?" he asked. "Can't you go in a straight line?"

"It's the current," I said. "This is on a direct line with the North Pole and so it polarizes the boat part of the time and we go in circles."

"Has anybody ever told you that you got a big mouth?" the littler guy said. "Row!"

So I rowed and we got to the island. We saw a lot of monkeys swinging from the branches of the trees, but naturally we didn't see Stam since he wasn't there.

"Do you know what I think?" said the moustache

guy to me. "I think you don't know your ass from a hole in the ground."

"I'll bet he isn't even Hamilton's brother."

"Yes—yes, I am," I said. "I can't help it if City Park is so big, can I?"

"Well, let's get in the goddamn boat and head back," said the big guy.

I wondered what they were going to say when they noticed there was only one oar. I'd thrown the other one in the lake as soon as we landed, and it should be floating in the middle about now. I knew I could get back to shore with one oar, but it would take longer. I wanted it to take longer.

"After we get back to shore," said the guy with the moustache, "let's take off. This is too damn much trouble just to get a guy to join the union."

"The union?" My voice broke, I was so shook. "Is that where you guys are from? The union?"

"Yeah, Parks and Recreational Workers. We got word to come out and talk to Hamilton about joining. I don't even want him to join—I never even want to see the sonofabitch."

So they weren't gangsters; they were union recruiters, and I'd been leading them all over hell and back for about two hours. And I'd even thrown away one oar of the rowboat so it would take us another hour to get back. But at least they weren't going to kill me when they found out. At least I wasn't going to get murdered.

I practically was, though, as soon as they saw that there was only one oar. "I wish we could throw this damn kid in the lake," the big guy said.

"Me too," said the moustache, "but you know it would give the union bad publicity."

"We could say he fell," said the big one, and I wasn't positive he was kidding.

"I'm really fast with one oar," I said. "I'll get you back in no time." And I did too, partly from joy that they weren't gangsters and partly from being so nervous at the dirty looks both of them kept giving me.

When we got to the shore, we walked over to where the car was parked and I started to climb in. The big guy put his hand against my shoulder.

"Forget it, kid," he said. "You're on your own from here."

"You mean you're not even going to give me a ride?" Not that I was crazy about them either, but I was a long ways from home.

"Here's a quarter." One of them tossed it to me. "Take a bus."

"It's forty cents for the bus," I told him. I didn't have any money at all.

"Jesus Christ," he said and threw me another quarter. Those union guys burned rubber getting away.

It took me another hour to get home across Denver on the bus, but I was pretty happy so I didn't mind that much. I was glad that nobody was after my brother— at least not those guys—and I was particularly glad on account of Tina. "You can count on me," she'd said. Wasn't that great?

She liked me, I really thought she liked me. I wished that I had a lot of money so I could buy her flowers and diamond earrings for her pretty little ears. I wished that I could see her smiling at me every day and that I was a big football hero so she could wear my letter sweater. Tina. Wasn't that a beautiful name? I was pretty sure I was in love with Tina, and I thought that I'd like to marry her when I grew up. But I knew somehow I probably wouldn't. I expect there are statistics to show that people usually don't marry the first person they love. This was something I wouldn't have forever, so I'd have to enjoy it while I had it. I hoped it would last until I got my driver's license at least.

chapter 5

STAM REALLY LAUGHED about the guys from the union, and I laughed with him, but I'll tell you it wasn't that funny when it was happening.

"You took them out in a rowboat and threw one oar away?" He shook his head like he couldn't believe it but did and really liked it. "I knew," he said, "when that girl, Tina, told me about those two guys, that you thought they were gangsters. You're okay, kid." He punched me on the shoulder, which meant he liked me.

"How did you like Tina?" I asked him. "Did you get her phone number?"

"For me or for you? Not bad," he said, "not bad at all."

"Well, did you get it or not?" I asked him. "I want to call her up. I thought you'd have enough sense to get it, for crissake."

"Oh, I had enough sense to get it," he said. He fished in his pocket and brought out a slip of paper with the phone number written on it and handed it to me. To this day I can still remember Tina's phone number. "She's old, you know," Stam said. "She's eighteen already."

"Well, I'll be sixteen the first of the year," I said, "and, besides, she doesn't know how old I am. You didn't tell her, did you?"

"Of course I didn't tell her. I got the plan as soon as she mentioned about you being a senior at Alameda High." He laughed. "Hey, do you really go for that girl?"

"She's okay," I said. "I just want to call her up and tell her thanks for finding you and giving you the message about those guys. I thought it was pretty important for her to tell you."

I didn't want to tell anyone that I was in love with Tina, not even Stam. I wasn't sure Stam had ever been in love with anyone himself; he sure never acted like it. Oh, he had lots of girls and they called him up a lot when they first met him; but usually when they got to know him, they got other boy friends. Because of the way he treated them—oh, not mean, just crazy. Very few girls like to be treated crazy I've noticed.

I've heard him call up more than one girl he had a date with and say, "This is the Happy Dale Mortuary. I just wanted to inform you that Stamford Hamilton is being interred here tonight. He died with your name on his lips, Judy." He always said "Judy," no matter what the girl's name was. And sometimes when they thought they were going dancing, he took them some-place like a meeting of the Denver Water Board, stuff like that. So he never kept his girls very long, but he didn't seem to care. No, I thought, Stam didn't know much about real love.

I wasn't really what you'd call an expert on it my-self, but I've had girl friends since I was in the fourth grade and gone steady twelve times so I wasn't what you'd call inexperienced. Except about actual sex, and I didn't know too much about that except what different guys said, and who knew how much of that was just bullshit? I kept thinking about Tina's pretty ears and her pale pink fingernails so I thought it was probably love. I'd never even noticed if she had a bust or not. Of course I figured she probably did or I would have noticed that. I thought her voice sounded like music, and I'd like to see her every day for the rest of my life. But I wasn't going to tell anybody that; it was just going to be my secret.

"So give her a call," said Stam. "As a matter of fact, she particularly asked me to let her know if you got home okay."

"She did?" She was worried about me, and she didn't even know me very well yet. Wasn't that great? "Well, I'd better call her up then, I guess," I said. "It's only polite."

Stam grinned, "And I know how polite you are. Look how you gave those two dumbos a guided tour of City Park." And we both laughed.

I called Tina the next morning as soon as I thought she might be up. I was ready at six, but I thought she might not be. I told her about those guys being union recruiters, but I didn't tell her I had thought they were gangsters. That was Stam's secret, and I wasn't going to tell anyone that, even someone I was in love with. I pretended that I had known all the time they were from the union, but Stam didn't want to join so I wanted to keep them from bothering him.

"I think it was wonderful of you," she said, "helping your big brother like that."

"He'd do the same for me," I said. "He's a pretty nice guy."

"He's awfully funny, isn't he?" she said.

See what a swell girl she was? Like I said before, a lot of girls think Stam is crazy instead of funny so I knew right away she was a very special girl.

"Maybe we could play some tennis sometime," I said, because it happens that I am almost as good at tennis as I am at baseball, and I wanted her to see me doing something I was good at. "In fact," I said like I'd just thought of it, "maybe you could come over to my house tomorrow night and eat supper and then we could walk up to the school and play tennis." I hadn't asked my mother yet, but since she always lets anyone who wants to eat dinner with us, I knew she wouldn't say no. And she didn't.

I got up early the next morning to clean the house for Tina. It's not that my mother can't clean house or that she's dirty. It's just that she won't throw anything out because what if it turns out to be something important like part of the toilet or somebody's car? A lot of the stuff is on the television set so when people come in, they will see it and take it away. Nobody ever does. There are about a thousand keys and any socks that don't have mates. On this morning that I was cleaning, I found a booklet titled *Your Career as a Meat Broker*. It's things like this that make you stop and wonder. At least they make my mother stop and wonder, and finally she just leaves everything and hopes for the best. What I did was put everything in a box and put the box under Stam's bed. I figured most of it was his anyway. Was he really thinking of being a meat broker?

I put all the baseball bats and gloves and balls in my room. I didn't know if Tina would come into my room or not. I hoped that she would so I put all the sloppy stuff in my closet and shut the door. I had an old pair of sneakers that smelled so awful I thought they might contaminate my closet forever so I tied a rope to them and hung them out the window. But what if Tina saw the rope and said laughingly, the way girls do, "Oh my, whatever is on the end of this rope?" And hauled them in and then fainted?

I finally took the sneakers outside and buried them under my window. I could always dig them up again, and I sure didn't want to throw them away. They were perfectly good except for the smell.

I would have liked to have the front yard fixed up

too with flowering bushes on each side of the front step and maybe some climbing roses going up the wall. All I could do was roll up the hose and sweep the walk. Mom vacuumed the carpet and scrubbed the kitchen floor because we were going to eat out there. We don't have a dining room either. We don't have a dining room or a basement, and this makes us practically refugees. I remembered then that Tina was poorer than we are and I thought maybe our house would look okay to her. At least it wasn't going to look weird because I had removed all the strange things. I knew my family was weird, but I didn't want Tina to know it. Poor is one thing; crazy is another.

Mom drove me over to Tina's house that afternoon to pick her up. Since I was supposed to be so old, I was kind of worried about my mom doing the driving, but I would just say I had lost my license almost as soon as I got it. Lots of guys do that, so I thought Tina would believe me.

"Why don't you get a girl in your own neighborhood?" Mom asked me as we were driving over to Tina's house, which was in south Denver. The only reason she'd been at Barkeley Park that day was because her grandmother lived in Lakewood. What a nice old lady, huh? "You never asked a girl to dinner before," my mom said. "You're only fifteen, Chance."

"I'd appreciate it," I told Mom, "if you didn't mention that to Tina. For some reason, she thinks I'm about eighteen."

"I wonder why," Mom said.

But I knew she wouldn't tell. My mother isn't bad at all. Actually, I really like her although I don't generally spread that around. When you're a teenager, you're supposed to hate your parents. Most of the guys I know can't stand their folks. I like my dad too.

"Guess what?" my mother said to me as we were driving along the freeway. "I'm writing a book, Chance."

Well, she has been saying she was going to write a book ever since I've known her. "Neat," I said, without getting very excited.

"No, really—I actually am," she said. "This time I am really going to do it. Remember when I told you about the book that would start out, 'There were violets in the snow that morning'?"

"Yeah."

"Well, this isn't it. I just loved that, but I couldn't think of anything to go with it. For a whole book you'd have to think of something to go with it."

"I think you're right."

"I'm afraid this book is going to have a plot and a regular story," she said and sighed. "I'd much rather write something that was great art, but I keep thinking of plots."

"You know, Mom, I don't think that's bad at all," I told her. "I think a lot of people like to read those kind the best."

"Oh, do you really think so?" She smiled. "I hope

you're right. And if I sell it, do you know what I'm going to do, Chance?"

I knew what I hoped she was going to do. I hoped she would get at least one thousand dollars and that she would give it to Stam to save him from the bookie.

"I am going to Rome to see Del," Mom said. "Wouldn't that be just wonderful? It has been six months since I have seen Del, and I've never seen Rome. I've never seen a lot of things."

If Mom gave Stam her money, she wouldn't get to go to Rome, and that would be too bad. I hadn't noticed that much that my mother didn't get to do very many things. Actually, I guess I never even thought that she wanted to. She was always cooking or typing or driving me somewhere or making up a bed on the couch for one of the guys. I guess I always thought that those were just the things she did. Period. And here she wanted to go to Rome. But I knew she would rather save Stam. Anyone would rather save Stam.

"I hope you sell it, Mom," I said. I wished I could tell her why it was so important for her to sell her book, but of course I couldn't.

"Well, don't tell anyone," she said, "or it might be bad luck."

And then we were at Tina's house. It seems like twenty years ago that I stood on the porch of Tina's house and rang her doorbell. But I can remember the way she looked as if it was only yesterday. White slacks that made her look nice and round but not fat. One of those little blouses that showed her flat brown stomach and had a ruffle below the roundness underneath that was Tina. It was a pink and white checked blouse and tied with a big bow in back. I never noticed girls' clothes at all until I knew Tina. "How do you like my new dress?" girls used to say to me and I would say, "Neat," or "Sickening," depending on the mood I was in or how I liked the girl. But I noticed Tina's clothes because she was in them. I can even remember that she had little gold rings in her ears and that her black hair had lights in it from the sun. I thought she'd probably just washed her hair for me, and I was proud. I thought that I would write a poem about Tina's hair. I never had that trouble before—wanting to write poems, I mean—so I knew I was really in love. I've always liked girls, but I've always been in control. Do you know what I mean? Well, now I wasn't. Writing poems about hair—I still had enough sense left to know that it was crazy.

"Hi, Chance," Tina said when she came to the door, and the way she said it made me glad that it was my name instead of "Herbert" or something that wouldn't have sounded half so great when she said it.

When Tina got into the car and I introduced her to Mom, I could see that Mom understood right away why I had said I was eighteen. That's why I get along so great with my mother and why I could never hate her even if I'm a teenager and supposed to. Because when it comes to the nitty-gritty, she's always there. And she didn't say anything dumb. She mostly talked about the weather, which is a nice, refined subject—isn't it hot, but it's hotter back east. All three of us sat in the front seat, so close together that when Tina breathed, I could feel it. I don't think I ever enjoyed feeling somebody breathe before.

As soon as we got home, though, everything started going to hell. The first terrible thing was Poppy's little orange car parked out in front of the house. Poppy is my grandfather, my mother's father. He is really crazy; he is seventy years old and a swinging single—honest! I hoped that Poppy would leave soon, but he said he'd come for dinner.

When I introduced him to Tina, he bowed and said something French. Tina's eyes were open wide like she'd never seen anyone like Poppy. Listen, nobody ever saw anything like Poppy, even on that TV show where everybody dresses up crazy to win prizes. He had on purple Bermuda shorts and an orange T-shirt that said "Yale." His legs looked like those birds that stand on one leg in the middle of lakes, and he had on orange sweat socks. "I've been to the health club," he said. "Marvelous, simply marvelous."

And he did a couple of deep knee bends and of course he fell over, and I had to help him up. What I would have liked to do was let him lie there, or better yet, roll him out the front door and leave him in the yard. But you have to act like you're kindhearted in front of girls. They would really hate it if you did things like roll old men out in the yard. I know they would.

Well, Tina was very polite to Poppy although I'm sure she didn't know what he was talking about most of the time. He speaks what he thinks is mod language but it is mostly stuff that nobody ever says like, "Boss," or, "Groovy," really silly stuff that nobody ever actually says.

Mom went out in the kitchen to finish supper and I went with her. "Please, Mom," I said, "please."

"I know what you mean, Chance," she said, "and I'm sorry. But what can I do—poison your grandfather? Try to remember that he is an old man."

"If he was an old man, I wouldn't mind," I said. "If he sat around nodding and mumbling and saying, Hey?, I wouldn't even mind that. But Poppy is just a—travesty. You know he's a travesty, Mom."

She raised her eyebrows at that and said, "Very good usage, Chance. Impertinent, impolite, but undoubtedly good usage. Now go back in the living room and take Tina out in the yard or something."

"Out in the yard? What for? To show her all the dog crap?"

"Why don't you show her where you buried your sneakers?"

So I went back in the living room just in time to see Stam and Jerry and Doug coming up the walk. As soon as they got inside, Jerry sniffed the air and said, "Ah, delicious," so I knew they would stay for supper.

Would there be enough? Would Tina get even one hamburger? I know that when lots of people come, my mother just makes the hamburger patties smaller, and once I found mine under the dill pickle, so small that it was hidden under the pickle. What if that happened to Tina? I decided that even if I didn't get any, I would see to it that Tina's hamburger actually had some meat in it. That's love, I'll tell you, when you don't even care if you get a hamburger or not.

Those guys had been out playing golf, and of course Jerry kept swinging his club around and clipped Tina on the ankle. When she said, "Ouch," he got down on the floor and started to rub her ankle and broke the strap on her sandal. He didn't mean to, of course; he just always does things like that. But since Tina had never seen him before, she was probably sort of surprised.

And Stam! I never saw him look worse. He had on a golf hat that was too little for him and said "Jack, the Ripper" on it, and he was wearing some cutoffs that might have been mine, they were so short. And his sneakers should have been buried too. But Tina just acted like Stam was perfectly all right. In fact, she was very nice to him, which showed what a nice, friendly girl she was.

Dad was taking a nap, and I prayed that when he got up, he would remember to put on his pants and zip up his fly. He says it hurts his stomach, zipping up his fly around the house. And Mom says that if he doesn't, she's going to start eating supper in her underpants. She didn't say anything like that the night Tina was over, though. She was very refined and tried to act like we were like other people although there was evidence all around that we weren't.

Some of the people had to eat in the living room on TV trays, but Tina and I got to sit at the table in the kitchen with Mom and Dad. Poppy was there too, and he was talking about *Last Tango in Paris* which was a dirty movie that was supposed to be art.

"It is a simple declaration of friendship," Poppy said. "When Brando sexually abuses Schneider, it is just his way of getting to know her."

I ask you, how many people's grandfathers talk like that? I'll bet Tina had never heard a grandfather talk like that.

"Relating to others," Poppy said, and he was practically yelling, "it's everything. Without communication, man per se is doomed." I thought he was going to fall over again.

Tina's head kept swinging back and forth from one person to another, and she practically didn't touch her hamburger, which I was sorry about since I'd given her half the meat out of mine.

Dad didn't pay any attention to anyone. He just ate his hamburger and read the ball scores the way he always does. Sometimes I think he does that so he won't go crazy with all the strange things happening around him. If somebody came in nude and painted purple, I think Dad would just read the ball scores. You know, you have to admire somebody as disciplined as that. I hoped Tina would notice what a normal-looking man my father was. He is gray-haired and paunchy like a middle-aged man is supposed to be. And then his glasses make him look quite dignified. And if you just saw him, you would think he was all right.

When the food was gone, so were most of the people. Mom says that's the way it always is. "It used to make me extremely bitter and distrustful of mankind," she says. "Now it just makes me happy."

I was happy when they were all gone too. I thought maybe Tina and I could sit quietly on the couch in the living room and I would act so normal, she would think the rest of the evening was her imagination. I was sort of afraid Dad would come in and turn on the television, which he always does even if there's nothing he wants to see. The TV set is my Dad's security blanket, I guess. No matter what happens around him, he knows he can depend on the old tube to be the same.

But Dad didn't come out. I could hear the radio playing in the kitchen so I knew Mom was making him stay out there. It was just like when she gives me an extra piece of pie because she says that I am still growing and need it. She was giving me some time to be alone with Tina because she thought I needed it.

I really liked it for a while sitting there like that with Tina. But pretty soon I began to feel like I should say something, and I couldn't think of a thing. I didn't want to tell her I loved her. I was only fifteen and I didn't want to get married or something. It's funny—girls usually tell me I've got a line that won't wait, and here I was on a couch next to probably the most beautiful girl in the world and I was struck dumb.

"So how about that tennis?" I said, and she said okay, so we walked up to the school where they've got lights on the court. I had planned to let her beat me as a kind of present from me to her, but I didn't have anything to do with it—she just beat me by herself. She was really good, and I was pretty surprised because I am good myself. But I didn't mind—her beating me. She could have hit me over the head with her racket and I would have just smiled. Well, I would have been pretty surprised, but I wouldn't have hit her back. I might not have actually smiled, but I wouldn't have hit her.

Back home, we had some Cokes and then Mom and I drove Tina over to her house. It was dark on her porch and while I was wondering whether I should kiss her or not, she just reached up and kissed me herself.

"I had a perfect time, Chance," she said. "I just love your whole family." Wasn't that nice? Wasn't she just the greatest girl?

When I got back in the car, my mom said, "What a nice girl. And she's so pretty."

"Yeah, she's okay," I said. I realized I hadn't thought about Stam's bookie once.

chapter 6

ALL OF A SUDDEN it was September. In Colorado in the fall the sky is such a bright blue you can hardly look at it, and everything is gold and red and a kind of silvery green. And the mountains are the most beautiful of all. The papers call it "Colorado's Color Show" each year when the aspen trees in the mountains turn.

Of course all these beautiful things are everyday stuff in Colorado in September and October until it snows. And it makes you glad every day and sort of sad too because it's kind of an end, and all the color is a death in a way.

It makes it hard to go to school when it is so great outside. But of course it was easier for me last year because I was finally in high school and pretty important. And there were some very nice-looking new girls too. Of course I had Tina so I wasn't too interested in any other girls, but a little bit. I was Class Rep last

year, which is short for Class Representative and that
means you are pretty popular and kind of a wheel. I
like things like that, I really do—and I don't know if
that means I am just ambitious or kind of disgusting.

There was a new guy in the tenth grade too, who had
transferred from a school in Denver. Oh, there was
more than one new guy of course, but this Harley Whitcomb really stood out. His clothes, for one thing. The
way it is, all the little kids in junior high wear their best
clothes, new clothes, to school the first week. But when
you're in high school, you don't. Because you're casual
by then, you know. Cool. So we all wore jeans with
bell bottoms, but not too wide. The bells were supposed
to be frayed on the bottom, and it wasn't fair to do it
with scissors because everybody could tell. And kind of
scroungy T-shirts with numbers on them like athletes.
Our sneakers were fancy, though, with colored strips
on them and made out of expensive leather like unborn
calves. My sneakers cost twenty dollars last year, and
my mom really screamed about it. Well, Harley Whitcomb's bells were so frayed, they were practically
scared, and his sneakers had stars on the toes! Everybody was crazy about Harley right away, especially the
girls, because he was pretty good-looking too. I didn't
like him at all because I was jealous. I wanted to be the
top soph guy, and I had a feeling that he did too and
that maybe he could. I think it's a good idea to admit
stuff like that to yourself, being jealous I mean. Be-

cause it's a lot easier to handle life if you know what kind of a person you are even if it's sickening. So I didn't like Harley Whitcomb, but otherwise, school was great.

I usually rode my bike over to Tina's house after school and stayed until almost suppertime. We sat on her porch in the swing and ate popcorn sometimes, and we talked about life a lot. Tina said that she thought a few years' difference in age between a man and a woman didn't matter that much, so I kind of wondered if she'd guessed I wasn't as old as she was and was trying to tell me it was okay. I would have liked to ask her, but I didn't say anything. I had it all planned when and where I was going to tell her. We were going to have the Homecoming Dance at Alameda the weekend before Thanksgiving. I had already asked Tina and she said that she would go. Somebody was going to be elected King of Homecoming, and his date would be Queen. I hoped that it would be me and Tina. I had a pretty good chance, I knew. My only serious rival was Harley Whitcomb. If I could make Tina a queen, surely she wouldn't mind that I wasn't almost eighteen, would she? I had great hopes for it so I didn't want to tell her yet how old I was. I worried about it a little but not a lot because I thought she liked me as much as I did her. Why else would she let me come over to her house every other night? I didn't take her that many places since I couldn't drive, and it is really embarrassing to have your folks drive you on a date. But we had a good time together. Sometimes we walked down to the neighborhood theater near her house to see a movie. We were just happy being together. Even now I think we really were. Tina didn't know it as well as I did, but I think she was happy. The way I felt—all the girls I'd had before, that had been baby stuff. I felt like I'd never had a girl before, but I didn't tell anyone how I felt about her, not even Stam.

Stam was still working at the park. He probably would be until it started snowing and even then, he might have to shovel or something. But he wasn't making very much money, nothing like the thousand that he needed. And he was always buying steak for the whole family out of his paychecks and new tapes for his stereo, stuff like that.

"What about the money?" I asked him once when we were alone. "What about the thousand dollars?"

"I don't know," he said. "Maybe they just forgot about it."

I didn't think anybody had forgotten one thousand dollars. They just hadn't found Stam yet. And when they did, what would they do to him?

If Mom would finish her book and sell it! I would tell her about Stam even if he told me not to because maybe it would save his life. But when I asked her about the book, she said that she had a long way to go.

"And probably I'll never sell it at all. I do have a good story though," she said. "I know it's good. Did I tell you about it, Chance, the girl who was a go-go dancer and then became a Jesus freak and finally married a missionary and went to Samoa?"

"No, I don't think you did, Mom, but it sounds good. Was your main character based on Sonia by any chance?" I asked her.

"No," she said, "why do you ask?"

"Oh, nothing," I said, "but there are a couple of things I could tell you about Sonia if you were interested."

"Such as?"

"Well, I don't want to go into details," I said. "Let's just say that if the spirit is willing and the flesh is weak, anything can happen."

"What do you mean?" Mom asked. "What in the world do you mean, Chance?"

"Let's just leave it right there, okay, Mom?"

"Listen, Chance, you're only fifteen," my mom said, as if that had anything to do with anything. I'll bet she's said that to me a million times except with different ages. I'll bet when I'm sixty-five, she'll be saying to me, "You're only sixty-five, Chance." Of course she might not even be around by then, which I'd rather not think about but it could happen.

"Relax, Mom," I said to her, "your baby boy is still *virgo intacta*." I wasn't sure that meant what I thought it did, but it sounded good.

"Oh, you!" Mom laughed nervously.

So she didn't have any money yet and might not for a while or even ever. And where was Stam ever going to get it?

Something happened next that made me think he was going to have to get the money from somewhere or head for the hills. It started with tennis; Jerry and I were going to play. He keeps trying to beat me just one time, and he never can. He thinks that because he is older than I am, and bigger, he should be able to beat me at something. But he can't—running, basketball, golf—I always trim him. Even when we play poker, I can beat Jerry—not Stam, but Jerry. If he didn't get so excited, he might have a chance. But old Jer really loses his cool. He breaks his tennis racket, throws his golf clubs, and tears up his cards. But he keeps coming back for more.

So we were going to play tennis this one Saturday morning that was September but nice and warm. We were going to City Park because Jerry had found a court there he thought was lucky for him, and he wanted to try me on it. On the way there we got a flat tire, naturally. When Jerry got the jack out of the trunk to change the tire, his spare was flat. Also naturally.

He kept looking up and down the street and frowning and shaking his head like he expected something worse to happen. Well, I didn't see what it could be. Because I really feel sorry for Jerry with all the bad luck he has, but I really hate it when I have it with him.

Because somebody has to think of something besides kicking the bumper.

"I don't like this, Chance," he said. "I don't like this at all."

"Hardly anybody would," I told him, "but it's not fatal. There's a service station on the corner and you can just walk down there and get somebody to fix the spare."

"Ha!" he snorted. "Do you know who runs that station?"

"Charlie Manson?"

"I wish he did," Jerry said. "I really wish he did, then I wouldn't be scared to go in there. I'll tell you who runs that station—the same guy who owns the bar next door to it."

"And you got thrown out of the bar because you poured your beer on the floor or punched somebody in the nose, right?" I said.

"That's Baby's," he practically whispered. "Remember Baby's?"

"You know I'm not old enough to go to bars," I said. "You're always telling me I'm only fifteen. How could I go to bars?"

"Stam," he said then. "The bet—the bookie. That's Baby's."

It was just like Jerry to have a flat tire practically in front of the place where he wasn't supposed to go, but I agreed with him that it wasn't good. So what were we going to do?

"Well, listen," I said, "why don't you just take a little walk and I'll take your spare down to that station. They'll think it's my car—nobody has to even see you. You go down to that hamburger place two blocks away and when it's fixed, I'll walk down and get you."

He actually smiled. "Yeah," he said. "Yeah."

So both of us got out of the car and just then the door to the bar opened and this guy came walking out, and he yelled, "Hey, Jerry."

"Keep walking," I whispered to Jerry so he did, but he looked kind of sick.

"Hey!" the guy yelled, and then he came running after us.

"It's him," Jerry whispered out of the side of his mouth.

Well, what could we do? We could have run, and I don't know about Jerry, but I could have gotten away from that guy because he had a beer belly that would have slowed him down some. But Jerry's car was there, and this guy had seen us getting out of it. So we had to stop.

The guy grabbed Jerry's arm and said, "What the hell happened to you? And that friend of yours? That guy dropped a bundle. And where do you live, buddy? And what's your phone number? And where does he live—this Stam?"

"Do you know what I think?" I said to Jerry then, and he shook his head. He was so scared, he couldn't even talk, for crissake. Well, I couldn't blame him, I really couldn't. I'd even been scared of union recruiters, and it was obvious this guy was the real thing, probably part of the Mob. "I think he thinks you're Jerry," I said to Jerry.

Jerry rolled his eyes back in his head like he was ready to faint so I shook him.

"It's simple, Terry," I said to him, "he has you mixed up with Jerry. It happens all the time," I said to the guy who was looking at me now like he wondered what I was trying to pull. And, believe me, I even wondered what I was trying to pull. Oh, I knew what all right—I just wondered why. Or especially how I thought I could get away with it. But I didn't know anything else to do.

"They're twins," I told this guy. "Terry and Jerry. Jerry is Terry's brother; this is Terry. I'll bet," I said to him, "you thought this was Jerry."

"I still think he's Jerry," he said. "In fact, I know damn well he's Jerry."

"I guess you're just going to have to take your pants down and show him your ass, Terry," I told Jerry.

He kind of gulped at that. I guess he figured he was in enough trouble without taking off his pants.

"You see, Jerry has this birthmark on his ass," I said, "and Terry doesn't have one. So that would prove he wasn't Jerry, right?" Yeah, it was pretty lame all right, but I hadn't had much time to think it out.

"Both of you come with me," old toughy said, and he took hold of our arms and started pulling us toward Baby's.

"No," I said, "I'm not old enough to go in bars."

He laughed out loud, and I saw one gold tooth glinting. Well, that cinched it as far as I was concerned. I've seen TV and movies, and I knew he was Mob now.

"What's the beef anyhow?" I asked him. "What do you want with Jerry anyhow? Terry here could give him a message." I stopped and planted my feet firmly with my knees bent a little so the guy couldn't pull me. I was only fifteen, but I was pretty strong. You can't do all the sports I've done all my life without getting strong.

"He knows," this guy said, tapping poor old Jer on the chest. "Old Jerry sure as hell knows."

"Well, what is it, Terry?" I asked him. "What's this guy got against Jerry anyway? Do you know?"

"I think it's something about a bet," Jerry mumbled.

"A bet!" I said like I was scandalized. "A bet? You mean gambling? Why, that's illegal," I said. "What are you," I said to the guy, "one of those bookies?"

Now it was his turn to look sick. "Not so loud, for crissake," he said. "Keep your goddamn voice down." So now I had found something he was afraid of. "I'm not a bookie," he said. "I—I just know this bookie, and he—well, he wants to see Jerry."

"Well, if this was Jerry," I said to him, "maybe it would be okay. But this is Terry. I'll tell you what I'm going to do," I said then, "I'm going to start yelling police in about one minute. In fact, that's my duty as a citizen. I'm going to call the police."

Well, I actually wasn't going to, on account of Stam. If I really did call the police, somebody might kill him for sure.

And I guess Jerry was thinking somebody might kill him for sure too, because he said faintly, "Oh, let's not do that."

"Both of you are coming with me," this guy said, and he started pulling us again.

"Have you ever heard of the statute about transporting minors for illegal purposes?" I told him, planting my feet more firmly on the sidewalk. "You're fooling with the Feds there, man. Because I'm a minor, and gambling sure is illegal."

"The Feds?" His voice almost broke, and I pressed my advantage.

"Yeah, Big Uncle. But listen, I don't want to get old Jerry in trouble so I'll keep my mouth shut except to tell him you want him when Terry and I see him."

"When will that be?"

"Tonight," I said. "He's coming over tonight."

"Where does he live?" asked the guy. "Where do you live? And how about this guy who made the bet? This Stam? Where does he live?"

"I don't know any Stam," said Jerry. "He must be a friend of my brother's." He was finally getting the idea.

"Well, where the hell does anybody live?" said this guy. I could see he was getting pretty tired of the whole thing.

"Do you think we'd tell you anything?" I asked him.

"Why, you're practically a gangster. You really should talk to your brother," I said to Jerry, "about the kind of people he knows."

"Listen, kid—I ought to—" He jammed an elbow in my ribs, or tried to, but I sidestepped it.

"I'm protected by the United States government," I reminded him, "and you'd better leave me alone."

"All right, goddamn it." The guy turned away. "But you—" He turned back to Jerry. "Jerry or Terry or Fairy—I'd better see somebody that looks like you in Baby's real shortly. Got it?"

"I'll tell my brother," said Jerry, "when I see him."

"And keep that kid's mouth shut or there isn't even going to be one of you," he said to Jerry as he walked down the street and slammed into Baby's.

Jerry and I didn't say anything after he left—we just broke into a dead run. We ran for about three blocks before we stopped and leaned against the wall of a store, gasping.

"What about the car?" Jerry said, choking.

"We'll just have to give some garage money to take care of the whole thing and drive it over to your house."

"Not my house," Jerry said. "I don't want to get my whole family rubbed out."

"Oh, yeah," I said. "There is that possibility, isn't there?"

It sure was sticky. I was even beginning to be sort of mad at Stam for getting into such a mess in the first place. But he didn't mean to, I knew that.

"Maybe you could just forget the car," I said to Jerry then.

"Forget the car?" He was yelling. "Forget my car, my goddamn car? Are you crazy, Chance?"

"I was afraid you'd feel that way about it," I said. "Well, I guess I'll just have to do it then. I'll have to get it fixed and then drive it home and if somebody follows me, I'll just have to lose him. I've seen it on those private-eye shows plenty of times; I think I can do it."

"You're only fifteen," Jerry said then as he usually did some time or other when he and I were talking. "You don't even have a driver's license. My God, do you even know how to drive?"

"Hell, yes, I know how to drive," I said. "What do you think I am—a goddamn baby?" Actually, I didn't know how that well. I had only driven once out in the country with my dad sitting right next to me, but I wasn't going to tell Jerry that. He was worried enough without me telling him that.

So that's what we did. Jerry gave me some money to pay for the tire, then he took a bus home and I took the spare down to that station and had them fix it. All the time I was changing it, I wondered if somebody from Baby's was watching me and would follow me when I left. But it seemed like when I pulled away that nobody was.

It's a lot harder to drive in traffic than it is on a country road, and I was really glad Jerry's car had an automatic shift instead of a stick. I think sticks are neater, but I didn't think it was a good time to learn how to drive one.

I never did see anybody I thought was following me, and once I almost ran into the car in front of me what with looking in the rear-view so much. But I took the long way home and went down lots of alleys and made sudden U-turns, stuff like that. It did occur to me that I would be in a lot of trouble if a cop stopped me and asked me for my license. I figured if that happened, I would say that my grandmother had had a heart attack, and I was the only one home and had to get to her, but I didn't think it would work as cops hear stories like that all the time. Fortunately, I never even saw a police car.

I parked about two blocks from our house just in case somebody had tailed me who I hadn't seen. Jerry was there already, and Stam. Nobody else was home, and I was glad. I particularly didn't feel like seeing my mom right then.

"For crissake, where have you been? Did somebody follow you? Where's my car?" Jerry asked me.

"I'm pretty sure nobody followed me," I told Jerry. "And your car is two blocks from here. But I'll tell you one thing," I was talking to Stam now, "you'd better start saving your pennies or Terry's twin brother is going to get creamed."

"I've been thinking about it," Stam said. "I'm just going to have to get another job where I can make some money. I really need some money," he said.

"It would be an advantage," I said.

chapter 7

SO WHAT STAM DECIDED to do was to go to an employment agency. "I've been looking in the papers all summer for somebody who wants an English major," he said, "and nobody does, so I am going to go to one of those places where they give you all kinds of tests to find the real you and what you should be in life. I would like to find the real me," he said.

"And also the thousand beanies," I reminded him.

"Yeah." He sighed. "I've got to get some money before Jerry wets his pants."

"He is kind of scared, isn't he?" I said. "He told me he was going to keep a baseball bat under his bed just in case."

Stam laughed. "He'll probably break his own leg with it if I know Jerry. Actually, he's safe enough if he stays away from the vicinity of Baby's because they don't know where his folks live and it's an unlisted number."

"How about his parents' company where he works?

Couldn't they find him that way?"

"It's not listed under their name," Stan told me. "It's Industrial Tools."

"How could I forget a catchy name like that?"

I was in a pretty good humor even if it was Monday because I wasn't in school. I had convinced Mom that going to an employment agency with Stam would be a good vocational experience for me. Actually, I'm not sure I convinced her because she said, "You're so full of b.s., Chance," but she let me go.

The name of the agency was Opportunities Un-limited, and it was in downtown Denver. "I like the sound of that," said Stam. "I might get to be head of a sugar plantation in Brazil or a beachcomber in Tahiti."

Opportunities Unlimited was on the top floor of a twenty-story building. So we knew it was an important place because the higher you are, the higher you are, if you know what I mean. The office had a front of copper glass, and inside it was red and black with zebra-striped furniture.

There was a good-looking blonde at the front desk and when we came in, she got a big smile on her face and said, "Stam Hamilton!" So she knew Stam, and that was good. It was the kind of place where you're glad if you know someone.

"Cecelia Bowen," said Stam. "Right?"

"Right," she said. "I haven't seen you since high school, Stam." And you could tell by the look on her

face she was sorry she hadn't. "Did you go away to
college?"

"I didn't exactly go away. I went to C.U. Denver
Center."

"Great," said Cecelia. "Men need to go to college to
get anywhere." And she smiled again.

Everything about her was just right, and you felt like
she'd planned it that way. Most girls do, I guess, but
some of them don't look like they did. Cecelia looked
like she did. Her teeth were so nice and straight, she
must have worn braces when she was about thirteen.
And she never ate chocolate or potato chips so her skin
would be smooth. Her hair color had a name, I bet, and
somebody in a beauty shop fixed it for her, puffing it
and flipping it and then spraying it with that stuff you
see on TV so it will stay even if you go out in a rainstorm. I doubted if Cecelia would go out in a rainstorm.
Or if she did, she would have an umbrella, and it would
match her raincoat.

"Do you want to fill out an application, Stam?"
Cecelia got up from her desk and went to a file cabinet.

Her dress was short, but not too short. She had pretty
good legs but not the kind to drive men wild. I had the
feeling Cecelia would not want to drive men wild. I
thought if Cecelia drove somebody wild, she would tell
him to fill out an application. Of course I didn't really
know any of those things. Guessing about people is just
something I do to pass the time.

Stam very seldom introduces people to other people so I said, "I'm Chance, Stam's brother."

"Chance?" Like she couldn't believe it. "Oh, you mean Chauncey."

"No, I don't," I said. "I mean Chance. That's my name."

She shook her head a little as if to say, well, all right, if you want to be that way. I guessed that Cecelia would name her children Jonathan, Edward, or Benjamin.

"Fill out this application," she said to Stam, "and then I'll have our Mr. Melcher give you the aptitude tests. Or do you know already what kind of a job you want?"

"No, I don't," Stam said. "That's why I'm here. What I want is a life work. It's kind of hard to find a life work when you're an English major."

Cecelia frowned a little and bit her lip with her even white teeth. "An English major? Oh, my, that is difficult. I wish you were a business major," she said. You could tell that she really did wish it too. "Oh, well, wait till you take the tests. There may be a few surprises in the tests. We use a computer, you know, and you'll find out all about yourself. There should be all kinds of opportunities for someone like you." And she smiled at him like she was one of them.

Our Mr. Melcher came out after Stam had filled out the application. He scurried out and bobbed his head at us and he kept looking over his shoulder like somebody was following him. I never saw anybody so nervous in my whole life. I guess if you looked a lot like a minnow, it would make you nervous.

"What?" he said to Cecelia. "What is it? You buzzed my buzzer," he said to her accusingly. You could see he just hated anyone buzzing his buzzer. He probably jumped about a foot every time somebody did it.

"This is Stamford Hamilton, Mr. Melcher," said Cecelia, "and he wants to take the tests."

"The tests?" Mr. Melcher looked like he was about ready to burst out crying. "Well, all right," he said. I think he hated people taking the tests about as much as somebody buzzing his buzzer. "You'll have to come back to the testing room," he said.

Stam and I both stood up to follow him, and Mr. Melcher shook his head like he was having some kind of a fit. "One at a time," he said. "You'll have to wait your turn, young man," he said to me. "Facilities for singles only in the testing room."

"What if you're married?" asked Stam.

"Oh dear," said Mr. Melcher, and he wrinkled his nose like he smelled something bad, "a sense of humor. Oh, my, that's bad—very bad for the tests. Well, try to control it," he said to Stam. "Maybe it will turn out all right," he said like he doubted it. And then he turned to me and pointed his finger at me. "Sit down. I'll call you when I'm ready for you."

"He's my brother," said Stam.

"I help him with the spelling," I said.

"Nobody can spell anymore," Mr. Melcher said like

it was a personal insult. "I don't know what they're teaching them in school nowadays. Can't spell, can't read, can't add two and two. Herman Hesse and Schopenhauer, that's all they know anymore. You can't help him spell," he said to me then, "because his spelling is part of his whole profile. The machine would take it badly, very badly, if he didn't do his own spelling. Who knows what might happen?" He shuddered like he thought the computer might just disintegrate.

"Well, okay," I said and sat back down. I sure didn't want to be responsible for blowing out a computer. I'd probably have to pay for it, and it might take my whole life. Actually, Stam could spell anyway; I just wanted to go in with him and see the tests.

So I had to sit there with sweet Cecelia for almost an hour. I walked down the hall and got a Coke. I couldn't go to the restroom because it was locked. Bathrooms are always locked in important places, because they don't want just any jerk coming in off the streets and crapping in the same place important people crap. I didn't really have to go anyway. I just thought I would to pass the time.

Cecelia typed on a red typewriter and every once in a while answered a red telephone, "Opportunities Unlimited," in a phony way. You could tell she'd practiced saying it; you could tell she was just in love with the way she said it. I was beginning to think old Cecelia was a real jerk. The way she held her hands on the typewriter like she was playing a baby grand piano, like she was a goddamn musician.

She didn't say much to me, but of course she had to ask me all the usual crap about how old I was, where did I go to school, did I like school. People could save a lot of time if they never said anything like that. I could tell that the only reason she was talking to me at all was because I was Stam's brother. I would probably be the last person in the world Cecelia would talk to if I wasn't Stam's brother.

"Stam isn't married, is he?" That was something she really wanted to know anyway.

"Not now," I said. Let her figure that one out.

"You mean he's divorced?"

"She died in an earthquake in Peru," I said. "But it's okay, Stam's still got the twins."

She was frowning about that when Mr. Melcher came back in, followed by Stam. Mr. Melcher was practically wringing his hands. "Never," he said, "never have I had anyone who was an introvert extrovert. It's impossible." He shook his finger at Stam. "Don't you know that's a flat contradiction, young man? No wonder the machine was disturbed."

"Well, I can't help it," said Stam. "I answered everything honestly. You said it was important to be honest, so I was."

"Look at this," Mr. Melcher held the test paper up and pointed at a line with his fingernail, "you answered

this one that you liked large parties and on the next
question, you said you preferred being alone."

"Well, I do," said Stam, surprised. "I like to go to a
large party and then afterward, I like to be alone.
What's so funny about that? I think that's a crazy test."

"It is not a crazy test!" Mr. Melcher looked like he
wanted to murder Stam. He came to about Stam's belt
buckle, and he looked like he was about to hit him.

"But what is he suited for?" asked Cecelia. "What
did the machine say he was suited for?"

"The machine became somewhat erratic," said Mr.
Melcher, "naturally, under the circumstances."

"But didn't it say anything?" asked Cecelia.

"According to the computer," said Stam, "I should
be a cruise social director at a forest ranger station in
the Catskill Mountains."

"It didn't say that! It didn't!" Mr. Melcher actually
stamped his foot. "It said, it said"—his voice broke—
"it said that he should have a job where he could be
alone among a lot of people."

"That's when you're really alone," said Stam, "when
you're with a lot of people."

"That's what I mean," said Mr. Melcher. "That's why
your test didn't come out right because you gave crazy
answers like that."

"But isn't there any kind of a job he would be suited
for?" asked Cecelia. "He has twins to support. He needs
a job."

"I don't have any twins," Stam said, and he looked

at me and laughed. "I'll bet Chance told you I had twins, didn't he?" He wasn't mad; he thought it was funny.

"And didn't you have a wife who died in an earthquake in Peru?" Cecelia asked him. She didn't think it was funny.

"No," said Stam. "But it doesn't sound any weirder than your lousy computer. I'm not going to pay fifty dollars to find out that I ought to be alone among a lot of people. I wanted a life work, not an ambiguous statement of an abstract philosophy."

"You college types are all alike," said Mr. Melcher, "just a bunch of smart mouths. You probably don't even have fifty dollars. You probably came here to take our tests when you couldn't even pay for them."

"I have fifty dollars," Stam said, "but I'm not going to give it to you."

He wouldn't either. If he didn't think he should do something, nothing could make him. They could throw him in jail or put lighted matches under his fingernails, he wouldn't do it.

"Get out of here!" Mr. Melcher shook his tiny fist in the air. "You have probably ruined our computer and practically given me a heart attack, and if I thought you had one red cent, I would sue you for it."

"Maybe I'll sue you," Stam said, "for misrepresentation. Good-bye, Cecelia," he added politely.

And he and I left. We went to a restaurant downtown and had chicken.

"You wouldn't believe that test," Stam said, "the kind of stuff we used to get in freshman psych in school. Things about sibling rivalry and do you masturbate regularly. If you were held up at gunpoint, would you fight or just hand over your money? I wouldn't do either one. I would try to reason with the robber. And if I couldn't, I would just walk away."

"What if he shot you?" I asked him.

"He wouldn't shoot me," Stam said positively.

Well, I hoped it would never come up. Because that is what Stam would do all right. He would just walk away.

"But what will I do now?" he asked.

"Why don't you just keep your job at Barkeley Park while you're waiting to find your life work?"

"Oh, I already quit Barkeley," he said. "It was only an interlude and the interlude was over. But I don't know, Chance—sometimes I get the feeling that something is pushing me and that I have to decide quickly. I don't know what in the hell to do, and something is pushing me. Oh, nobody is saying anything to me, but I have this feeling that I have to do something pretty soon. It's really a terrible feeling. I hate feeling like that."

"Don't worry about it," I said. "You'll find something, Stam. Maybe you could go back to school and get a master's and be a college prof like Mom wants you to be."

"If I went back to school, I'd take East Indian philosophy," Stam said, "and I'd take geology. Nothing that made any sense, just things I'd like to know. Maybe that stupid computer was right, maybe I really am crazy."

"You're not crazy, Stam," I said, and that was one thing I was sure about. My brother was different, but he wasn't crazy. I hated hearing him talk like that because I halfway agreed with him, not that he was crazy but that he ought to do something pretty soon. But what was it going to be? What should someone like Stam be?

"Are you ever going to call that Cecelia?" I asked him then, to change the subject but also because I wanted to know.

"Why would I call her?" asked Stam.

"She wishes you would," I said.

"Well, I'm not going to."

chapter 8

BUT CECELIA called Stam—the next morning—and she said she had a job for him. Her father owns a big men's store downtown, and he was going to give Stam a job. She said that if Stam would meet her for lunch, she would tell him about the job and take him over to the store to talk to her father.

I didn't think he was going to make very much money working in a store, but he said that he could. He told us all about it at supper that night.

"I will get a commission on everything I sell," he said, "and since they charge a lot of money for everything, I should make a lot too. I will have to wear a gray flannel suit and a white shirt," he added.

Stam in a gray flannel suit? He likes clothes like jeans and T-shirts that say "WHAT?" on the front. "That's really terrible, Stam," I said to him.

"I have to give it a try," he said. "Who knows? Maybe that's where my place is—in Bowen's Men's Store."

I could hardly stand it when he said that. Stam in a suit and a white shirt? How could anything like that be Stam's place.

"Mr. Bowen is a member of the chamber of commerce," Stam said, "and he wants me to join too."

All of us stared at him. Stam a member of the chamber of commerce? It was about as crazy as Stam in the Gestapo.

"You can get your hair styled and wear after-shave lotion," I said to him. The way he looked when I said that made me ashamed of myself.

"Hair doesn't make any difference," he said.

But I knew that it did. He didn't want to get his hair cut or wear a suit. He didn't really want to work in a store and join the chamber of commerce, but he thought that he should. It was the first time I had ever known Stam to do something because he thought he should. Did that happen to everybody? Was it going to happen to me? It just made me feel like hell.

"A lot of guys look really neat with their hair styled," I said to him.

"I'm going to get it cut, Chance," said Stam, "not styled—just cut."

So even if he had to go that way, he wasn't going to go any farther than he had to. He was still going to be Stam, wasn't he?

"I am going over to Tina's," I said after we finished eating. I really felt a lot like seeing Tina.

"Now, Chance, you know I don't like you riding a long way at night on your bike."

"I'll give him a ride over," Stam said, "and then pick him up later. I am going to have a few beers to celebrate my new job."

To celebrate or to drown his sorrow? I was going to try not to even think about it. That's why I was going to Tina's. When I was with Tina, I didn't think about anything except her.

And it was the same as it always was except even better, because we were all alone.

"My mom's out on a date," Tina said. She didn't say it sad or mad or anything like that. Just said it the way she would say that her mom was at the store or something. But maybe she wanted her mother to go out on dates so that she could get a new father.

It seemed kind of sad to me. I couldn't imagine my mom out on a date with anybody but my father. And I couldn't imagine ever having any father but him. But these things happen. It had happened to Tina, hadn't it? I sure hoped I wasn't going to grow up to be the kind of person who couldn't cope with sad things. Look how bad I felt about Stam getting a job in a store and having to wear a suit. And here I was practically breaking up because Tina's mother was out on a date.

Tina and I were sitting on the couch in her living room, and the fact that it was an old couch with the stuffing coming out didn't make me feel any better.

Listen, we don't have a lot of money, but the stuffing isn't coming out of any of our things. Except me. I sort of wondered if the stuffing was coming out of me, worrying about things so much. Maybe Tina would be better off if she did get a new father. At least he might buy them a new couch.

"What would you like to do?" Tina asked me then. She was looking just as pretty as she always did in white shorts and a green blouse that buttoned down the front. Somehow that made me feel worse, her looking so pretty and being poor and not having a real family.

"I don't know," I said, and then I thought of the sprinkler on the lawn. It had been a hot day even if it was the end of September, and it was still warm in the evening. "Let's go out and run through the hose," I suggested.

"Run through the hose?" Tina frowned at me for an instant like she thought I was crazy, and then she said, "Well, all right, if you want to. We can run through the hose, I guess, if you can't think of anything you'd rather do." She said it sort of like she was mad at me. I thought maybe she'd hoped I was going to take her to a movie or to get a Coke or something.

"I don't have any money, Tina," I told her so that she'd know I wasn't just a deadbeat who didn't know any better. "Maybe my brother will give me a few bucks next weekend. He's got a new job, and I'll bet he'll be glad to give me a little money."

So Tina wanted to know all about Stam's job, and I filled her in on all the details, including Cecelia Bowen.

"Do you think Stam likes Cecelia?" she wanted to know.

"I don't think he likes her at all," I said.

"Well, maybe he will have to go with her whether he likes her or not," Tina said, "since she is the boss's daughter."

"Stam wouldn't do that," I said. "That would be just like—like being a gigolo."

"Is she pretty?" Tina asked.

I thought about it. "Yes, I guess she is pretty. If you like the type," I said, "which I don't." Not wanting Tina to be jealous.

"Is she as pretty as I am?" Tina asked me. It wasn't conceited, it really wasn't. It was kind of cute, the way she said it.

"Nobody is as pretty as you, Tina," I told her. It was the truth, but it made Tina smile. When she smiled, she had a little dimple that twinkled just for a second at the corner of her mouth. It was so fast that you'd miss it unless you were looking for it specifically. I was always looking for it.

"Since you really do think I am pretty," Tina said, "I will run through the sprinkler with you." Aren't girls funny?

We had a really good time that September evening, splashing water on each other and getting soaking wet.

I could see the dark moving into the sky and the early evening stars.

"When I was a little kid," I told Tina, "I thought the stars were little holes in the sky that let the lights of heaven through."

I'd never told anyone that before, and for a minute I was sorry I'd told Tina because she just said, "That's sweet," real fast the way girls do when they don't mean it at all.

But then I forgot all about when I was a little kid and stars and everything because Tina giggled and said, "Look how wet I am." And I did.

With the porch light on, I could see her very plainly, every bit of her. Because with her shorts and her blouse plastered to her, Tina was practically naked. I just stared at her for quite a long time even though it was a very impolite thing to do. But I felt like I couldn't move.

Finally I said, "You'd better go in the house and take off your clothes." As soon as I said it, I realized how terrible it sounded, but Tina just laughed.

"Come on," she said and went up the steps and onto the porch.

"Oh, I'll wait here," I said. It did seem like the thing to do.

But Tina said again, "Oh, come on—you're wet too. You'll catch cold, Chance."

"Well, okay," I said, "I'll come in the house, but I

didn't bring any other clothes with me." I was going to keep my clothes on even if they were wet. For one thing, my shorts had a hole in them.

In the living room I sat down on a wooden rocker which didn't seem that bad if it got wet.

"I'll just be a minute," Tina said and she went into the bedroom.

I thought she'd come back with some regular clothes on, but she had on a robe when she came out of the bedroom. A long, kind of silky red robe that really did look very nice on her. It was one of those kind that tie at the waist and if you untie it, the robe just opens up. I tried not to think about that.

Tina sat down on the couch and she shivered, "I'm freezing," she said. "Come sit by me and get me warm, Chance."

Well, I wanted to and I didn't want to, if you know what I mean. But it didn't seem like it would be very polite of me to say no, so I did.

Tina snuggled up next to me and put her head on my shoulder, "Put your arm around me, Chance," she said.

"I'll get you all wet," I said. "My shirt's wet."

"Yes, it is," she said. "Take off that wet shirt, Chance."

"My shirt?" And my voice broke the way it does when I get excited, which I was doing. "Take off my shirt?"

"I'll help you," she said, and she began to unbutton my shirt. Her hands were very warm for someone who was freezing.

"I guess I'd better go home, Tina," I said. Because she couldn't know how I was feeling, the terrible things I was thinking. Tina was a very nice girl, I reminded myself. Just because she was cold was no reason for me to turn into a sex maniac. I buttoned my shirt again. "I'd really better leave," I said. "I've got dry clothes at home," babbling like an idiot, "and I'd better go."

"I thought you liked me, Chance," she said against my ear, and she was very close to me.

"Oh, I do, Tina. I really like you. I—I practically love you." I'd never said it before. "I do love you, Tina." The first time in my life I'd ever said that to anyone. I can still remember when I said that to Tina.

"Kiss me if you love me," she said.

Her lips were sweet and warm, and I could feel the softness of Tina under her robe. I put my arm around her. She kissed me again, she moved in my arms, and my hand touched her breast. I didn't mean to do that. It was an accident, my touching her like that. I tried to move my hand, but I couldn't. I could feel the nipple of her breast, and I couldn't move my hand.

Tina made a funny sound in her throat, kind of a moan or a gasp. I thought I must have hurt her, or at least hurt her feelings. I knew it was a terrible thing for me to do, but I hadn't meant to. I didn't even know how it had happened. I jumped off the couch and tucked my shirt in my jeans.

"I'm sorry, Tina—I'm really sorry. You just don't know how guys are, Tina, but I've got to go home."

She looked up at me and her eyes were bright like she was mad. "You make me sick, Chance Hamilton," she said.

Her robe had come open clear down to the waist, and I could see the tops of her breasts. I felt terrible staring at her breasts like that when she didn't even know I was doing it. I felt terrible, period.

"Listen, Tina," I said, "I wish I could explain all this to you, but you're too nice a girl, you really are. So try not to be too mad at me."

She didn't say a word, just kept sitting on the couch staring at me like she'd like to hit me.

I walked to the door and then I turned around. "Stam is coming by for me later so just tell him I walked home. Okay?" It was going to be a long walk home, but I was looking forward to it, I really was. Our P.E. teacher always says exercise is really good for sexual frustration.

And by the time I got home, which was two hours later and I had to stop along the way for a milkshake for energy. I felt better. I thought that Tina would get over being mad at me. After she thought it over, she would know that I hadn't meant to be fresh with her. I wouldn't have done anything like that to Tina for anything. When you really care about a girl, you protect her. Raping her sure wouldn't have been protecting her, which I actually felt like doing. It scared me to think how much I felt like doing that. One other thing would have stopped me, besides protecting Tina, I mean. I

wasn't exactly sure how to go about it. Oh, I had a
vague idea, but I thought I'd look awfully dumb while
I was trying to figure it out. And I would never want
Tina to think I was dumb. I would rather she would
think I was noble. Which I sure hoped that she would
after she thought about it.

Stam came home about an hour after I did, and I
heard him go into his room. I went right in and said,
"Did you stop by Tina's? Is she mad at me?"

"I think she did mention it," Stam said.

"Well, she'll probably get over it," I said. "After she
thinks it over, I'm sure she'll get over it."

"Why don't you get another girl, Chance?" Stam
asked me then. "Get a girl your own age. Tina is really
too old for you."

"I might just do that," I said, keeping it cool.

I wasn't about to tell Stam I didn't want any girl but
Tina. He'd think I was crazy, letting a girl get to me
that way. He can take them or leave them, he really
can. But then Stam wasn't in love with anybody the way
I was with Tina. Being in love can be wonderful even
if you do get hurt.

chapter 9

FIRST, I THOUGHT I would call Tina up on the phone and then I figured it would be too easy for her to hang up on me. So I just decided to go over to her house after school the next Monday and throw myself on her mercy. After all, I hadn't really done anything to her, had I? I had thought about doing something, that was true; but I hadn't actually done it.

I rode my bike over to Tina's that Monday, and Tina came to the door when I rang the bell. When she saw me, her eyes got wide like she was afraid of me, and she said, "I don't want to talk to you, Chance."

"Please let me come in, Tina," I said. "I have something important to say to you."

"Well, what is it about?" she asked me, not moving out of the door.

"You and me, Tina. It's about you and me."

"Oh." She looked at me for a long second and then opened the door so I could come in.

"First of all, Tina—" I said. I was standing up in the middle of the floor and I felt like I was making a speech so I sat down on the rocker. "First of all, let me say that I have only the utmost respect for you." This was something I'd read in a book once and it seemed to fit in.

She smiled then. "I know," she said.

"Well, then, why are you mad?" I asked her. "If you really do know that, why are you mad? You know everything if you know that. You know why I wouldn't take off my shirt and why I went home. So why are you mad, Tina?"

"Who said I was?" she said.

Just like that. I'll tell you—it's really hard to figure girls.

"So come on out in the kitchen," she said, "and have a Coke. My mother isn't home, but it's perfectly safe."

"You're always going to be safe with me, Tina," I said. "You can count on that."

"Yes, I can count on that, can't I?"

I couldn't figure her out. She still acted like she was sort of mad at me, talking in a cool tone and not ever really looking at me. Well, I figured she'd get over it. At least she hadn't thrown me out.

We sat at the kitchen table with our Cokes, and Tina passed me a bowl of pretzels. "You're not really eighteen, are you, Chance?" she said to me then.

"Not quite," I said. "I suppose Stam told you."

"No, he didn't tell me," she said. "I just kind of figured that you weren't."

I thought it was time to change the subject. "Stam started his new job today."

"Oh, did he?" she asked. "How is Stam anyway?" Still in that cool tone like she couldn't care less about anything I said.

"Cecelia is having him over to dinner tonight," I said. "You remember me telling you about Cecelia, the one who got him the job?"

"Oh, yes," she said, "the boss's daughter. How nice for Stam. And you said she was pretty too, didn't you?"

"I said she wasn't as pretty as you."

She really looked at me then and smiled, one of her dimple smiles. "You really do like me a lot, don't you, Chance?"

"Yes, I do, Tina," I said. "Quite a lot."

"So you can still come over to see me," she said, "and I will come over to your house too."

"And don't forget the Homecoming Dance just before Thanksgiving," I said. I hoped I was going to be King and she would be Queen and it wouldn't matter about me being young anymore.

When I left, I kissed her good-bye and she let me, which was more than I expected. Then she reached up and touseled my hair. "I don't know anyone nicer than you," she said. Which meant that she liked me a lot too; I knew that it did.

So I already felt good by the time I got home and after I got there, I felt even better. Because my dad had gotten me a job, a real job. Not a paper route but a real job—busboy at Sojo's. Sojo's is a restaurant in Lakewood, and my dad knows the guy who owns it. Joe Sotell, the owner, has a little girl in my dad's fourth grade at school. Joe said I could work two nights a week and weekends. I was going to make two dollars an hour, so maybe I could help Stam a little. Well, I said a little, didn't I?

Two nights later, when I went to my job for the first time, I wasn't quite that glad. Because I had to wear dark pants and black shoes, and I didn't have any so I had to wear Stam's, and he was about three times as big as I am. My pants were up under my arms, and my feet felt like they'd died somewhere in those big shoes. Plus I had to get my hair cut. So there I was scalped and wearing big black things. But I was working!

I guess most people hate working. They talk about blue Monday and the TGIF club, which means, "Thank God It's Friday." But the first time you get a job, it's great, you feel like a man. It's practically like being in love with somebody for the first time. It's sort of the same kind of feeling because it's the first time you've done that too. Doing things you've never done before and are scared to do but then it turns out all right, and you know you are going to get paid for it. I loved my job. The paper route didn't count; that was for little kids who wore braces and collected baseball cards.

In my job I cleared all the dishes off the table after people ate, filled the coffeepot with water, mopped the kitchen, and did whatever else the cook wanted me to. Another busboy worked the same shift I did. His name was Seppi, and he was Italian. He was very cool and showed me how to do everything. When I made mistakes at first, he covered for me. I dropped some glasses and he got the broom and helped me sweep up before the cook saw it. He helped me carry the heavy coffeepot.

I'd never known anyone like Seppi before, and if I hadn't gotten my job, I probably never would have. Because when you live in the suburbs, you only know people like you. Which is stupid, because you never learn anything if everybody is just alike. After I got to know Seppi, I decided that I would try to know as many different people in my life as I could. Remember how I told you all the people in Lakewood have basements? Well, Seppi's family lived in an apartment in north Denver, and there were seven of them with only two bedrooms! But he said they had a good time all the time. Seppi's real name was Guiseppe, and he was seventeen; but we were friends anyway.

When you work with somebody, you're a different kind of friend than with somebody you've known all your life. Like John McKay. I've known him since we were in kindergarten, and I used to put paste in his hair. We played in my sandbox and made roads for our toy cars and trucks. Then we had wrecks. I got my whole thumbnail torn off when we had one of our wrecks. When we went to school, I had a lunchbox with The Beatles on it, and he had Bozo the Clown. When we were in the first grade, John wet his pants right in front of the whole class. He cried, and I almost cried too because he was my friend, and it was practically like it happened to me.

But, like I say, Seppi and I were a different kind of friends. We were more men friends because we had jobs; and, besides, Seppi was older than I was and really cool. When he got through work, he put on tight yellow pants with zippers up the side, and ankle boots that were black and white patent, and I mean he was ready to cruise!

Seppi had a big black motorcycle too, and one night after work, he asked me if I wanted to take a trip. That's just how he said it, "Do you want to take a trip tonight, buddy?" You know what I thought at first, don't you? Yeah, I thought he was going to give me some dope. "We'll really fly," said Seppi.

"I don't know, Seppi," I said to him. "I don't care much for tripping."

"Tripping?" He grinned. "What do you think, Bonzo, I'm a head or something? I don't do that shit," he said. "I'm gonna be a big star, I don't got time for that stuff. I mean a trip on my bike," he said. "A real trip on my bike. I gotta go up to Morrison to see this girl who works at the Dairy Dish there. I thought maybe you'd like to ride along."

I said that I would and I told him I was sorry for what I'd said about tripping.

"Think nothing about it, kid. Let's go," he said. "Get the lead out, okay?"

Well, I had to call my mother and tell her I'd be late or she might call the police or at least, my boss. "I'll have to make a call first," I told Seppi and went into the booth in front of the restaurant. I sure as hell wasn't going to tell Seppi I was calling my mom. He might not even let me go if he knew I was the kind of a guy who called his mom when he was going to be late. Hardly any of the guys I know do that, but it really doesn't hurt anything, does it? So I called her and told her I was going to ride up to Morrison with a kid who worked at Sojo's. I didn't mention the motorcycle; Mom really hates motorcycles.

Personally, I would rather have a motorcycle than a car even. Because you are whizzing along in the outdoors and you can feel the wind and see the sky above you and the road unwinding under you. All that power, all that speed—you feel like a god. Now it was October, you know; there was a big, golden moon in the sky and we sped up hills and down hills and around curves. Sometimes it seemed that we went so fast, the wind reached in my mouth and took my breath away. I really liked it. I liked it so much that I had to yell. Seppi yelled too, and we went down the road yelling and laughing with the wind streaming the noise out behind us, scattering our yells and our laughs all over the countryside.

Morrison is a little town in the foothills, about six miles from Lakewood, and we made it in twenty minutes. But when we got to the Dairy Dish, Seppi's girl wasn't there.

"Stupid broad," he said. "If she's stepping out on me, I'll cream her. Or better yet, I'll get another broad." He nudged me in the ribs. "That's what to do, hey, kid? If one dame puts you down, get another one. The world's full of broads, right? So we'll get us a malt and sit down by the stream, okay? It's a nice warm night to sit down by the stream and we can have some conversation about life and stuff."

The Dairy Dish sat up on a little hill overlooking a winding mountain stream. Of course it was dark, but we could see the lights from the drive-in sparkling on the water through the trees that grew on the hill.

We sat at a table and drank our malts and after Seppi had come to the bottom of his, he wiped his mouth and said, "Did I tell you I was going to be a big star, Chance?"

"You just mentioned it," I told him. "Just in passing, you might say."

"I'm going to Hollywood," he said, "and get in TV.

That's where the money is—in TV. Next month I will have five hundred dollars in the bank and I'm taking off on my bike for Hollywood."

"You want to be an actor, huh?" I asked.

"Oh, actor—" He shrugged his shoulders and smiled. "I don't want to be an actor, just a leading man. I want to be one of those sexy guys that are always in bed with a broad or else shooting somebody. You know, like Clint Eastwood or that Al Paissano."

"Pacino," I said, "Al Pacino."

"Yeah, him. I can do what those guys do. Look tough or sad or sexy. I can look sexier than either of those two guys." And he showed me how he could look sexy.

Well, he really looked stupid. But of course, me not being a girl, maybe I wasn't a good judge.

Besides, how did I know? Maybe he really would get to be a big star. My mom says that you can be anything you want to. When I was a little kid, she told me all the things I could be if I really wanted—a scientist, an artist, a doctor—anything in the world I wanted if I would only try.

"I've been getting ready for a long time," Seppi said. "Looking as handsome and sexy as I can and not eating potato chips because of pimples. I practice the expressions I will need in front of the mirror—love, hate, sadness, and happy."

He did his expressions for me, one right after another —so fast that I about laughed. But I didn't, because what a guy wants to be is not a funny thing, and his friends shouldn't laugh.

I told Seppi that I had kind of planned to be a ball player but didn't know if I was dedicated enough. "I don't just play ball every minute like I probably would if I was a natural. Sometimes I like to do other things like ride my bike or just lay down on the grass somewhere and let things happen around me."

"And girls," said Seppi, " you like girls, huh?"

"Doesn't everybody?" I said.

Well, it was really nice. All of a sudden we were good friends, and I felt like I could talk about almost anything to Seppi. Oh, not Tina—I didn't want to talk to Seppi about Tina. Because to Seppi, girls were broads, and to me, they weren't. We were just different. It's easy to be friends with someone who is just like you, but being friends with someone who is different is more interesting because you find out a lot of things you didn't know before. I knew I could even tell Seppi about Stam's thousand dollar bet and maybe he would have some ideas.

"A bookie, huh?" he said and shook his head. "Jesus, those guys'll kick the crap out of you."

"So what can he do?" I asked him. "Could you think of a way my brother could get a thousand dollars?"

"The finance company?" he suggested, then he shook his head. "Hell, no, the finance companies are worse than bookies. And the interest! They'll suck your blood, the bastards. I could tell you about my old man," he said, "but you don't want to hear about my old man. Even my old lady don't want to hear about my old man. The only way to get that much money is pushing and dealing."

"You mean drugs?" I asked.

"Yeah," he shook his head sadly, "I mean drugs. Or running numbers—all that kind of stuff that can give you a ticket to the pen. That's why I'm going to be a big TV star, so I can get rich without getting in the rackets."

"My brother wouldn't want to get in the rackets." I was sure of that.

"Hey," Seppi said then, "maybe you could sell your body."

"You mean, be a whore?" I asked him.

Seppi started to laugh and he laughed so hard he fell off the bench next to the table and lay on the ground gasping for breath. I had never seen anyone laugh so hard, and I thought maybe he was having some kind of a fit. I thought maybe he was just going to choke to death, laughing that hard.

Finally he sat up and wiped his eyes. " 'You mean, be a whore?' " he mimicked me. "No, you crazy sonofabitch, I mean sell your body for after you're dead to a medical school or somewhere. Or let your brother sell his. He's bigger than you, huh? Maybe a big body would bring more."

"Can you do that?" I asked him. "How do you do that?"

"Sure," he waved his hand confidently, "sure, you can sell your body. My old grammaw did that. The old lady was hardly cold before all these places started coming around for her parts."

Well, I didn't much like the idea of people coming around for my parts after I was dead, and I thought my mother would like it even less. But Stam really needed a thousand dollars. "How do you do that?" I asked Seppi again. "Who should I call to find out about doing that?"

"Call Information," he said. "Information knows everything."

I decided I would do it the next day when I got home from school.

chapter 10

BUT WHEN I CALLED the Information operator the next day and asked her where a person would go to sell his body, she thought I was crazy. She started giving me this speech about "nuisance calls are prohibited by law. Apprehension of persons making such calls may result in imprisonment or loss of phone service."

"Do I get my choice?" I asked her.

"What is your number?" she asked me foxily.

"I'll never tell," I said and hung up. I hoped she couldn't trace the call. But I hadn't actually done anything, had I? For a second there, I had been a victim of the 20th Century Fear of Authority. It is there in almost everybody, I guess, just buried more deeply in some. I'm not actually afraid of anybody, but when someone starts talking about apprehension and imprisonment, I get a sort of uneasy feeling. My mom says that if ever a cop came up and pointed his gun at her and asked her if she did it, she would say that she did even before she found out what it was.

After I thought about it for a while, I decided that the logical place to sell a body would be a medical school. Those interns are always cutting up bodies, everyone knows that. So I called the C.U. Medical Center and asked the Information girl there. At least she didn't seem surprised. But she gave me another extension, and I wondered if it was going to turn out to be the Psychiatric Center. I never did find out what department it was, though, because this woman just answered with her name.

"Mrs. Saunders," she said in the kind of voice that is supposed to be soothing but usually makes me suspicious. When somebody uses that tone to me, it usually means that they are humoring me. But I went ahead and told her what I wanted. I figured there wasn't any law yet against asking questions. "What you are contemplating is illegal," she said in the same sweet tone.

"I wasn't exactly contemplating it," I said. "I was just wondering. Actually, I'm writing a book," I said, having just thought of that, "and my main character sells his body so that this poor, little crippled girl can have an operation. See, she'll die if she doesn't have it and—"

She interrupted me. "Of course donations can be made to the eye or kidney bank but must be accompanied by a physician's form attesting to the soundness of such organs."

"Oh, my organs are sound," I said. It was only my

mind that was going. I knew that she and I were both thinking that. "I'll think about it," I said. "I'll give you a call if I feel like donating anything."

"You have to be eighteen," she said then. So how did she know I wasn't? My voice hadn't broken once. Her saying that really pissed me off, and I hung up without saying good-bye.

Why was I so damn worried about the money anyway? Stam sure didn't act like he was. I hardly ever saw Stam anymore. When I did, he didn't even look like himself, coming in at suppertime in his suit and white shirt. And Cecelia was always calling him or having Stam over or coming over to our house. I didn't know which was worse. Well, actually, it was worse having her at our house because she acted like we were all crazy. When she talked to any of us, especially me, she enunciated very clearly, the way you do when you are talking to a deaf person or someone from a foreign land. So I talked back to her the same way, which made our conversations very tiring.

"What's with Cecelia?" I asked Stam one night after he'd been at that job for about two weeks and had seen Cecelia almost every night.

"She just seems to go with the job," he said.

"Because her father is your boss?" I asked.

He smiled at that. "Oh, you mean the old American success story. No, not because her father is the boss. Because the kind of a guy who would have that job would have a girl like Cecelia. It just fits. It has nothing to do with what I like or don't like. It has something to do with balance," he said.

"It has something to do with insanity," I said, but he just shrugged.

Cecelia called him Stamford. Wasn't that sickening? What if he married her? I thought maybe joining the Establishment was the worst thing that ever happened to Stam, maybe even worse than owing a bookie one grand. Because the worst thing that could happen to him with the bookie was getting bumped off. I figured marrying Cecelia would be even more terrible because he would never get away from her and it would be a fate worse than death. But he sure didn't seem to be worrying about the money or Cecelia either.

And so far nobody had found him. Jerry said that he didn't think anybody was after him either, or at least he never saw anyone following him. He drove to work a different way every day and took another route home at night. After he got over being scared, I think Jerry sort of enjoyed it.

"I didn't even know there were so many ways to go," he told me one night when he was over at our house, "and so many people and all kinds of neighborhoods. After this is all over, I think I will still go places as many different ways as I can. It keeps a person from getting in a rut, don't you think so, Chance?"

"Or even a grave," I said, and Jerry shuddered. He hadn't quite gotten over that time at Baby's yet.

So to hell with it, I thought. Why should I sweat the

money if Stam didn't? I thought I probably would though whether I wanted to or not.

But it was time for the carnival at my dad's school, and I was going with him. I meant to have a good time too. I always go to school activities with my dad because it seems that he gets a kick out of it. And it doesn't hurt me that much. Dad always gives me five dollars for the carnival, and I go to the baseball throw and I buy pie and I finally end up in the room where they show old cartoons.

Anyway, I figured it would take my mind off my problems—Stam's money, Cecelia, and Tina. Oh, Tina wasn't really a problem. I still went to her house and she called me on the phone when I didn't, or I called her. I figured if she didn't really like me, she wouldn't call. But she was different, and I didn't know why. Oh, I guessed it was because of sex. When sex enters in, a relationship changes. I read that in a book too, and it sure seemed to be true. It made me feel sort of bad even though we did still have a pretty good time together.

And if I got to be King at the Homecoming Dance, things would be better, I knew. It was mostly because of Tina that I wanted to be King. I hadn't told her yet that I was only a sophomore; I planned to tell her the truth that night, that I was only fifteen instead of eighteen. But almost sixteen! I would be sixteen after Christmas, and maybe that would help. Also if I were

King and she got to be Queen, I knew that would help a lot. Most girls really go for stuff like that. The girls in the home ec classes were making the purple robes and the golden crowns. They were going to paste jewels on the crowns, but not real ones.

Tina—that was one reason I wanted to be King, but also because of the way it would set up the whole year. Once you get to be a king, people just naturally start thinking of you as pretty important, and you get to be a lot of other things too. At the end of the year our school holds elections to see who is going to be what, and I wanted to be president of the junior class the next fall. Things like that really help when you're trying to get a scholarship, which I would be. A scholarship to Dartmouth or Yale or Harvard. Everybody thought that was crazy, and my dad said he would send me to Colorado University, which is a good school and has been known to beat Oklahoma in football, and you know what that means. But I didn't think it would hurt to try for the Ivy League. So it was important for me to be King of the Homecoming Dance.

But going to the carnival with Dad was going to be just for fun. And it really was. They had more good stuff than they'd ever had, even a Trip to the Stars room where they showed slides on all four walls at once, and you felt like you were traveling through space. Naturally, I won a lot of prizes at the baseball throw, but I gave all of them back except for a beanie with a propeller on it. I figured since my dad was a teacher there, it wouldn't look too good for his son to take all the prizes.

I bought an apple pie from a lady at one of the bake tables, but I could only eat half of it since I'd had a pretty big supper. Then I watched some really ugly little girls doing the hula in a room they called Beauties of the Islands. Which made me head for the cartoons. Listen, Minnie Mouse looked great at the side of those hula dancers.

After I watched a lot of old cartoons, I went in the cafeteria and had a cup of coffee and the rest of the pie. My dad came in then with a bunch of other teachers and it took about fifteen minutes for them to say I was getting bigger and to kid Dad a lot and for him to kid them. His principal even kids him. Everybody really likes my dad.

So then we were ready to go home, and I took the beanie with the propeller that I'd won at the baseball throw and gave it to a little kid walking down the hall.

"That was a nice thing to do," Dad said to me.

I just shrugged. "I might be getting a little old for propellers," I said.

He looked at me for a minute like he was surprised at what he saw, and then he grinned. "Yeah, I guess you are at that."

I have a pretty neat father, I really do. Oh, he runs around in his underpants and hates rock music, but he is an okay guy just the same. When he and I got home from the carnival that night, Dad and I sat at the kitchen table and had a beer. Yeah, I had one too; my dad gave it to me.

And the neat part is the way he did it. He just opened the refrigerator and said, "I'm going to have a beer. How about you, Chance?"

"Okay," I said, "I don't mind if I do."

He didn't say a word about me being really too young and that he hoped I wouldn't become an alcoholic because of his giving me a beer. He just handed me the can.

"Hey, how about the Broncos?" he said.

"This is going to be our year," I said.

"Can't miss," Dad said.

The Denver Broncos, that's our football team. I guess everybody everywhere knows about the Denver Broncos.

"Football's great," I said then, "but baseball—that's my game. I guess I like baseball better than anything."

"I'm with you, kid," Dad said.

"I might want to be a ballplayer when I grow up," I said.

Dad looked pleased. "Well, now, I didn't know that, Chance. That's great, boy—hope you make it. It takes a lot of work, you know."

"Dedication—that's what Stam says. Stam says I'm not dedicated enough."

"Time will tell," Dad said. "That used to be what Stam wanted too. Maybe he's getting you mixed up with himself. That happens all the time. Sometimes even I"—he chuckled—"I get myself mixed up with you guys, being young and wanting things. It doesn't seem so awfully long ago that I was a hotshot on the Pueblo Steelies and sure I would make the pros before I was twenty."

"What happened?" I asked him. "I mean, how come you didn't?"

Dad spread his hands and shrugged his shoulders. "Who knows? Not good enough, I guess—or dedicated, like Stam says. Time goes so fast, Chance, and suddenly it seems that it's not what you're going to be, but what you are. So I'm just a schoolteacher." He didn't say it sadly but sort of humorously like it was some kind of a good joke on him.

I didn't think it was a good joke; I thought it was terrible. When he talked that way, I felt a chill like a cold wind was blowing on me. I was afraid. My dad had wanted something just like I did, and what had happened to him? What would happen to me?

"I guess you must be a really good teacher, Dad," I said to him, wanting it to have turned out all right for him. "All the kids calling you Mr. Ham and coming back to see you when they're grown up and wouldn't even have to. All the kids like you a lot."

I love you, Dad. It's what I was thinking; it was what I wanted to say. But I couldn't. What kind of a fifteen-year-old kid tells his dad out loud that he loves him?

But he knew. None of us in our family says stuff like that, but all of us know.

"It was all meant to be," Dad said like he was talking to himself. Looking at all the things he'd wanted and what he had. It was sad as hell, I'll tell you.

"Did you know my favorite team was the Dodgers?" I said then like I'd just thought of it. "Stam still talks about when you and he went to Los Angeles and saw Koufax pitch against St. Louis."

"Does Stam still talk about that?" Dad grinned. "We had a good time then, Stam and I."

"I was just a little kid then," I said, "and I didn't get to go. I hardly even knew what a baseball was."

"But you do now, huh, boy? We'll have to pitch you a few, Stam and I. Hit you some grounders if you want to be a ballplayer."

Those were the things Dad said that night and what I think he meant was that Stam and I were his boys, and he was going to help us all he could.

What if I told Dad about Stam and the money? Maybe he could think of something. But what would it be? My dad doesn't have any money, I know that. That's one reason he is sort of ashamed of himself— because he doesn't have money. In America you're just shit if you don't. Look at the way poor people get pushed around—people on welfare, old people. I hate stuff like that, I really do. Sometimes I think when I grow up, what I want to do is be nice to all the people everyone else is mean to. I don't feel like that all the time. Most of the time what I want is to be rich. Then I could be even nicer. Right? But rich people hardly ever are, have you noticed? Who was the nicer guy—my dad or Uncle Al? See what I mean? When I was little, I remember Dad talking about how much money we were going to have when he got to be a principal. Principals make a lot more than teachers, I guess. But I hadn't heard him talk about being a principal for a long time. I guessed he had given that up just like he gave up being a ballplayer.

So what could he do about Stam? Nothing. And it would make him even more ashamed of himself than he already was. Sometimes I get the feeling that my dad is lonely—lonely right in the middle of the whole family. That's a crazy thing, I know. We all talk to him, and he talks to us, but somehow he doesn't seem to be part of it all. Sometimes he acts like he's surprised to find himself here with all the loud music and the craziness and all the people. He reads the paper and listens to music of the Forties on the radio. He watches TV and talks about sports, but still he is mostly by himself. Why is that? Is a man that way if he doesn't get the things he wants in life? Were the things he had enough —being a teacher, having a family? I wanted my dad to be happy. I didn't want him to be alone.

"Hey, Dad," I said then, "remember that song about 'Take me out to the ball game'? That's a pretty good song, isn't it?"

He smiled and he began to sing the song, " 'Buy me some peanuts and crackerjack—' "

" 'I don't care if I never get back,' " I sang it with him and we went straight through the whole song. Drinking beer and singing together—my dad and I.

chapter 11

OCTOBER WENT BY so quickly; I can hardly remember it. Stam was still working at Bowen's store and going with Cecelia. I worked at Sojo's weekends and went over to Tina's whenever I could, or whenever she said I could. A lot of times she had to study, and so did I. I want to get good grades so that someday I will be a big success. If I read all the books and do all the assignments and get all *A*'s on my report cards, I am practically guaranteed to be a big success. But will I find out anything that I want to know? There are so many things that I want to know—about heaven and reincarnation and why southerners talk slower and who decided that twelve inches would be called a foot? Was it a guy whose own foot happened to be twelve inches long or a famous mathematician named Mr. Foot? Why does A love B instead of C? Or what makes your stomach ache when you're homesick? What's the use of being a big success if you don't know what makes people laugh? Dogs can't laugh; cats don't even want to. Exactly what is a laugh anyway—I mean in physical terms? And why do some people think a certain joke is funny and other people say that's the stupidest thing they've ever heard?

When I go to the library for extra-credit reading, I spend practically the whole time talking to this old guy who stands at the door and looks at your books to make sure you're not trying to rip off any. This old man is from England and came to the United States to live with his daughter in Denver, but he is very homesick and likes to talk about England. He can tell about the fog and the queen and the moors with heather on them. Some of the old castles there have real ghosts, he says, and London is a "proper fair city." He can tell me more about England than any book in the library. Right? On the other hand, I might like to have a boat and a camper and a split-level house with a swimming pool. So I am going to get good grades just in case.

I meant to save some of my money from Sojo's to help Stam out, but it seemed that I was always spending it on Tina, trying to make everything the way it was before. Trying to fill up the empty feeling I had with hamburgers and fries and malts, trying to get one of her dimple smiles by taking her to a funny movie. Sometimes I felt like she was getting older all the time, and I wasn't. Sometimes it seemed that I wasn't ever going to catch up with her even if I got to be the King of

Homecoming and she was the Queen. But it would be all right then, I told myself. It would have to be all right then.

So I never had any money to give Stam, and I didn't know if he had any either. I guessed that taking Cecelia out all the time wasn't helping his financial situation any. She was the kind of girl you'd have to take to real fancy places that cost a lot of money. What was the matter with him anyway? Stam hates places like that. Stam doesn't even like girls like that.

"It couldn't be sex," I said to my mother one morning when it had gotten to be November and it was snowing and nothing seemed to be getting any better.

"What couldn't be sex?" asked my mom, and she handed me a piece of cinnamon toast, which was golden and bubbling.

A lot of times when it's a lousy day, Mom gives us good things to eat. And it helps, it really does.

"Sex?" she said again. "Not in the morning—okay, Chance? I don't want to talk about sex in the morning. I'll get you a little booklet or something about the birds and bees instead."

Well, she was only kidding, I was pretty sure. The birds and the bees—Christ Almighty.

"What I really want to talk about," Mom said, "is why Jerry wants to move in with us. He says it would be safer. How could anyone say it's safer here? And it certainly won't be safer with Jerry here. We'll all have to watch out for flying debris, broken bones, and so on."

"Hmm," I said, not really wanting to talk about it. I could guess why Jerry wanted to move in with us. He had seen someone from Baby's or thought he saw someone, which was more likely, knowing Jerry.

"And someone keeps calling here for Stam," Mom said, "and then hanging up when I ask who it is so he can call back. What's going on anyway?" she asked.

"Girls," I said vaguely. "You know how girls are."

"It isn't girls," Mom said definitely. "You don't know if Stam and Jerry are in some kind of trouble, do you, Chance?"

"Mom, you know those guys are crazy," I said. "But speaking of sex," I said, trying to get the conversation turned in another direction.

"Which we weren't," Mom said.

"I was talking about Cecelia," I told her. "Why is Stam wasting his time on a deadhead like Cecelia anyway?"

"Who knows?" Mom made a face. "Why does he do any of the things he does? Why is he working in a store in the first place? And wearing a suit all the time? I never thought," she said, shaking her head, "that Stam would turn out to be Establishment."

It's not that my mom is a member of the radical Left. It's just that she's a writer. Writers always hate the Establishment.

"Well, he had to have a job, didn't he?" I asked her.

"Why didn't he go back to school and become a professor?" Mom asked. "Stam would be a wonderful professor. And he wouldn't have to wear suits all the time. He could wear old tweed jackets with leather patches on the elbows."

"Maybe he thought he couldn't afford to go back to school," I pointed out to her.

"He could have worked his way through grad school, couldn't he, by stoking the furnace or something?"

"Mom, you don't stoke furnaces anymore," I told her. "And maybe Stam doesn't even want to go to grad school, did you ever think of that? Actually, Mom, education is practically as phony as business. All that talk about rapport and cultural enrichment and sensitivity—that's just a bunch of bullshit. You know that, don't you, Mom? All that fine talk—it doesn't mean a damn thing. Every kid who makes it through high school knows that."

"I thought it would be wonderful for Stam to be a professor."

"You thought it would be wonderful," I said to her. "That doesn't mean he thought it would be wonderful. You're not us, Mom. You have to come to grips with that one of these days."

"Touché, kid," she said. "I'm getting there. Bear with me. I'm in kind of a metamorphosis right now. I'm in the process of turning from a mother into a person."

"Oh, yeah?" I said, grinning at her. Actually, I like her as a mother pretty well.

"Yeah," she said. "And the book is doing it. I am actually writing the book, Chance, after all the years

of just talking about it. I wasn't sure I could do it—
that's why I just talked about it. But I am doing it. This
week I am sending out queries and outlines to publishers."

"Do you think you'll make a thousand dollars?" I
asked her, thinking about Stam again.

"A thousand dollars?" she looked puzzled.

"Well, you probably would, wouldn't you?" I asked
her. "And there might be something that you could use
it for that would be pretty important. You know?"

"Going to Rome to see Del." Mom smiled. "If I do
sell it, I will go to Rome all by myself and be a person
for sure."

Well, what could I say to that? It would be really
great for Mom to be a person instead of just a mother.
I would miss her just being Mom, but she couldn't be
that her whole life, could she? Especially after all of us
were gone. When we were all gone, it would be better
if she was a person instead.

And, besides, she'd never get the thousand dollars in
time to save Stam. How was Stam going to be saved if
he couldn't save himself? Who had been calling him on
the phone anyway, and why was Jerry wanting to move
in with us?

"Listen, Mom," I said then, "how about me staying
out of school today?"

"Are you sick?" she asked. "Where's the thermometer?
Is it your throat? Do you have a sore throat?" See, she
wasn't a person just yet.

"I'm not sick," I said, "but I would kind of like to go downtown and see Stam. Maybe he and I could eat lunch together. I never get to see Stam anymore by himself. I would really like to talk to him a little."

Mom smiled, "I know what you mean, Chance. You miss him, don't you? Miss him while he's still here? Yes, you can go," she said. "You go down and have lunch with Stam. I'll call the school and excuse you. Find out if he's all right. I worry whether or not Stam is all right. But I try not to think about it; I am trying to think about my book."

"You have the right plan, Mom," I told her. "You're going to be a real person."

"And, listen," she said, "I want you to tell Jerry he can't move here. Safer? That's just crazy. I don't have time for craziness anymore, Chance. You tell him—or better yet, I'll tell him myself."

"Mom," I said, "I think you're really going to make it."

So I went downtown on the bus to eat lunch with Stam at noon. I was really lucky because Cecelia had a sore throat that day and wouldn't be eating with us. If she had been, I think I would have gone home because I was in no mood to be treated like an idiot child whose nose is running.

Stam was glad to see me. He didn't ask me what I was doing there or why I wasn't in school. That is one of the best things about him. He never asks people why they are in one place instead of another. He can see that they are, and that's enough for him.

"We will go to this place I know where they have great hamburgers and beer," Stam said. "Of course I can't have any beer because Mr. Bowen doesn't like the salesmen to drink on their lunch hour."

Tough shit, I thought, but I didn't say anything, just followed Stam down the street to Ms. Fred's, which you have to admit is a screwy name for a hamburger joint. It wasn't exactly a joint because the hamburgers cost two dollars, and it was easy to see why Stam didn't have any money if he went to places like that all the time.

We sat down and ordered hamburgers and fries and after the waiter had gone, I said to Stam, "The heat's on."

He laughed out loud and said, "What's that supposed to mean?"

"Mom says an unknown person is calling you all the time and hanging up, and Jerry wants to move in with us because it's safer."

"Oh," he said. "Oh, yeah. I haven't seen Jerry so I don't know what's bugging him. Probably thought some kid on a bike was a hit man in disguise. But I know about the phone calls because I was home one night when this guy called."

"And?"

He nodded his head. "Yeah, it was Abe all right."

"Abe?"

"Abe, the bookie," Stam said. "That's not his real name of course. I think his real name is Shark or maybe Killer."

I felt like I could hardly breathe. It had finally happened, the thing I'd been afraid of all along. They'd finally found Stam, and now what were they going to do to him?

"What did Abe say?" I asked Stam.

"He said that he would like to see me soon."

"Maybe you could borrow the money from Mr. Bowen," I said. "He must be a pretty rich man, and I'll bet he likes you since his daughter likes you."

"I don't think Albert Bowen likes anybody," Stam said, "and I especially don't think he likes giving people money. I can hardly even get my commissions out of him."

"Well, why don't you quit? If you can't make the thousand dollars there, why don't you quit?"

"Because it's real life," Stam said. "Everything about it is so boring, I figure it must be real life. Being bored is very reassuring because it's something you can count on not to change."

Of all the crazy things I'd ever heard him say, this had to be tops, and I said so. "That's weird."

"No, Chance, it isn't weird," Stam said. "That's the beauty of it, don't you see? It's normal to be bored. Our whole economy is based on boredom. Look at television, education, thousands of laws and government regulations—even food. Do fresh tomatoes actually taste like tomatoes anymore? They taste like water or soybeans. Traffic is boring. Everything." He smiled. "I have it all figured out, Chance. Normality is boring."

"But you're not normal, Stam," I said. It wasn't what I meant exactly, but he nodded his head like I'd pleased him.

"You know that," he said, "and I know that, but I am doing my best to keep it a secret from the rest of the world. When I really put my mind to it, I can be just as boring as the next guy."

"Migawd," I said. "And how about Cecelia?"

"Ah, Cecelia." He shook his head fondly. "Cecelia is, perhaps, the most boring of all. Do you know, Chance, that I can tell, almost to the exact words, what she will say about any given subject. I can foretell with uncanny precision how Cecelia will react to any given situation. Fascinating," he said, "absolutely fascinating."

"What about Abe?" I asked him. "And the thousand dollars?"

Stam frowned. "Now there, I'll have to admit, we are deviating from the norm. That situation doesn't seem to fit into real life. I don't know exactly what I am going to do about that." He shook his head, "I think I am going to have a beer after all," and he signaled the waiter.

"What about your boss?" I asked him. "I thought Mr. Bowen didn't let his salesmen drink at lunch?"

"What Mr. Bowen doesn't know," said Stam, "won't

hurt me." As soon as the waiter set the bottle down, Stam took a big gulp of it. "American businessmen turn to alcohol in moments of stress," he said. "It's as normal as apple pie, in case you were wondering."

"What I'm really wondering," I said, "is how that bookie got your phone number."

"Yeah, me too," said Stam. "I'll bet old Jerry had something to do with it somehow."

"Jerry wouldn't do that," I said. "He's your best friend."

"Jerry would do anything," Stam said. "Jerry wouldn't mean to do it; he might not even realize he was doing it. But you know how he is."

I thought about Jerry for a minute. "Yeah," I said.

"Oh, well," said Stam, "they don't know where I live. I still have time." He looked at his watch then. "And speaking of time, I'm late for work. Mr. Bowen doesn't like his salesmen to be late either."

"Why don't you call in sick?" I suggested. "Say you got a bad case of food poisoning at lunch. Did you know the Marx Brothers were on at the Flick in *Animal Crackers*?"

"*Animal Crackers*." Stam smiled. "My favorite one." He shook his head then. "I couldn't, Chance. Cecelia would kill me when she found out."

"Are you scared of Cecelia?" I asked him.

"I'm trying to be like everyone else," he said.

That was a funny kind of answer, but I knew what he meant.

As we were walking down the street toward Bowen's store, Stam said, "You might as well come along with me, Chance, and see the store. You've never gotten to see the store." So he didn't want to go back alone.

"Sure," I said, "I'd like to see the goddamn store."

Mr. Bowen came bustling up to us as soon as we came in the door. I would have known him anywhere because he looked like his daughter. Oh, not as pretty as Cecelia, and he didn't wear his hair like hers, but he had the same smug, fat little mouth.

"Well, Stamford," he said, "what happened to you?" He raised his nostrils then like he smelled something bad. "Have you been drinking, Stamford? You know we don't tolerate that at Bowen's."

"I had a beer," Stam muttered. I had never seen Stam act like that before, and I just hated it—kind of ashamed of himself and looking down at his feet.

"Oh, well," said Mr. Bowen, "don't let it happen again. Mr. Sylvester is here about his slacks. He says they're too long. Try to remember, Stamford, that Bowen's customers do not wear high-heeled shoes. Bowen's clientele is mainly Old Guard and likes trousers that break beautifully at the instep." He was just as big an asshole as his daughter. "Who is this?" he asked suddenly, glaring at me.

"This is my brother, Chance," Stam said. "He wanted to see the store."

You could just see the wheels going around in Mr.

Bowen's head. First of all, you could tell that he didn't like my looks since I was a teenager and had longer hair than he did. But, on the other hand, if his daughter married Stam, and I thought she planned to, that would make us sort of related. And, besides, he liked people to see his store. He just loved his store, you could tell.

He spread his arms out wide then and said, "Well, here it is—Bowen's. Twenty-five years." Like it was his marriage. "Kind of makes you stop and think, doesn't it, young man?" he said to me.

Yes, it did. It made me stop and think that this could happen to Stam—twenty-five years in this big, rich morgue. You could tell that all their clothes cost a lot and all of them would be terrible and you wouldn't even wear them to your funeral if you could help it.

"Go ahead, son," said Mr. Bowen in what he probably thought was a kindly manner but which really left me cold. I don't like being called "son" by people who aren't my father. My own father doesn't even call me that. "Look around," Mr. Bowen said to me, "just don't deter Stamford from his duties."

"Oh, I don't think anything could deter Stamford from his duties," I said. I could tell by a gleam in the back of Stam's eyes that he thought it was funny. So he wasn't gone yet.

Stam went over to the suit department where a short, fat man was standing in front of a mirror looking at himself. First at his front and then at his back. Neither side was worth looking at, believe me. I don't know which was biggest, his stomach or his butt.

"There you are," the man said crossly to Stam. "Taking bankers' lunches, are you?"

"I hope you haven't been waiting long, Mr. Sylvester," Stam said politely. I was standing behind a rack where I could see and hear but not deter.

"Now that you've finally gotten here," said Mr. Sylvester, " do you think you can manage to do something about these ridiculous pants you sold me? Look" —he pointed to his fat, little feet—"they cover up my shoes."

"Longer slacks are the style, sir," said Stam. "But of course Bowen's will be glad to make any alteration you wish."

"Well, I wish," said Mr. Sylvester, "I certainly do wish. When I got them home, I was just shocked. Shocked," he said.

"I did think when you bought them, Mr. Sylvester, that you should try them on," Stam said. "If you'll remember, sir, I suggested that."

"Same size I've worn for years," Mr. Sylvester grumbled. "Why should I try them on?"

"Because they're making slacks longer now," Stam said, still being polite. "That's why, sir."

"Well, get your chalk or whatever," the fat man said. "They're almost a foot too long, that's for sure."

"No problem," said Stam and he went behind a

counter and came out carrying a big pair of scissors.

"But I thought you used chalk. Don't you mark them with chalk for the tailor?"

"That's for small jobs," Stam said, and he squatted on the floor at Mr. Sylvester's feet and began to cut the pants with the scissors. "When it comes to a matter of feet rather than inches, we have to use bold measures." He cut off a big piece of material halfway up the man's calf and then sat back on his haunches. "There," said Stam, "that's about a foot."

"What are you doing?" exploded Mr. Sylvester, looking at his bare leg in the mirror.

"Hold still," said Stam, digging the scissors into the other pant leg. "I wouldn't want to cut you, sir." He cut this side even shorter than the other and sat back again to look, his head cocked to one side like he knew just what he was doing.

"Hey!" Mr. Sylvester bleated. "Stop that now, do you hear? Have you lost your mind? What are you doing?"

"Shh," said Stam with the scissors back in the first pant leg, "I'll just have to even these up. You wouldn't want to go around with one leg shorter than the other, would you? A man in your position—people would talk." And he kept cutting, first one leg and then the other with Mr. Sylvester yelling and squeaking but afraid to move, until those slacks hit that fat man at the knees.

I was sticking my face in the rack of the sport jackets now to keep anyone from hearing me laugh. You've never seen anything so funny—it topped everything else

Stam had done in his whole life. And it was like a terrible weight had rolled off my shoulders, him doing that.
Because he was going to be all right after all.

"Well," said Stam then, "is that short enough, sir?"

"Mr. Bowen," the man yelled at the top of his lungs.
"Mr. Bowen!"

Mr. Bowen came scooting up, breathing hard and
looking like he was about to have a fit of some kind. Nobody had yelled like that in his store in twenty-five
years, you could tell that.

"What is it?" Mr. Bowen asked. "What's going on
here? Mr. Sylvester, what—" He stopped and looked at
the fat man in the short pants. "Good God," he said, and
you could tell it wasn't swearing, it was praying. "Merci-
ful God," he added.

Stam just stood there, the scissors still in his hand and
that nice, polite smile on his face. I've seen that smile
before, right after he has done something that somebody wants to kill him for.

"Mr. Sylvester," said Mr. Bowen, like he was about
to cry, "how can I ever—is there any way—? Any slacks
in the store, Mr. Sylvester—anything." He looked at
Stam then; his face turned almost purple and veins stood
out on his head. "Get out of here! No pay. Those slacks
you've ruined will take care of your pay. Never—
never—" His voice was breaking. "Don't ever let me see
you here again! That goes for my daughter too. Cecelia
is through with you. Do you understand? Through!"

Stam smiled. "If you say so, sir," he said.

I came out from behind the coat rack then, and Stam and I walked out of Bowen's store.

"We still have time to make the movie," I said.

"I'm always going to see the Marx Brothers," Stam said, "whenever I can."

chapter 12

JERRY WAS THERE when Stam and I got home from the movies. He was sitting out in the kitchen drinking a cup of coffee, and nobody else was home.

He gave us a sad look when we came in. "What's the matter with Lora anyway?" he asked and then went on before we could say anything; "She won't let me move in. All these years—she's never said I couldn't move in before."

"Mom's trying to turn into a person," I told him.

"Oh," he said, "Women's lib. That explains it. Ever since women got the vote, they've been getting more uppity all the time. And here I am in danger, real danger, and your mom won't even save me."

"What's the matter?" Stam asked him. "Did somebody follow you? Did one of those guys from Baby's find you?"

"Nobody exactly found me," Jerry said. "It's more

like I found somebody. I don't know what we're going to do, Stam—they're everywhere."

"Where did you find who?" I asked Jerry.

"At Big Jim's" he said. "I thought I was safe at Big Jim's—it's clear on the other side of town from Baby's —but guess what? The bartender from Baby's—you know, Keetch? Keetch, the guy who knows me? Well, he's tending bar at Big Jim's now. I almost died on the spot." Jerry clutched his heart and rolled his eyes. "I don't think Keetch saw me, but maybe he did. Maybe he fingered me and somebody tailed me. They're everywhere, Stam. Jesus Christ, what are we going to do?"

"How did Abe get my phone number?" Stam wanted to know.

"Abe? Migawd, do you mean Abe? You mean the bookie, Abe?"

"Yes," said Stam, "one and the same. I was just wondering if you knew how old Abe got my phone number."

"That girl!" Jerry clapped a hand to his head. "Migawd, that girl! So Keetch did see me, and that girl was a plant. But she was a real doll, Stam. She looked just like the kind of a girl who would want your phone number."

"Oh, I think she was," Stam said. "I think she really was. She wanted it all right, to give to Keetch to give to Abe."

"She came up to me in my booth," Jerry said, "and she sat down and gave me a big smile and I was pretty happy. I am always hoping something like that will happen to me, and it never has before. 'Hi, Jer,' she said, so I figured she knew me even though I couldn't remember her. And then we talked for a while and I bought her a drink and I was trying to make the moves on her when she said, 'I've lost Stam's phone number— you know it, don't you, Jer?' So I gave it to her and pretty soon she went away. Believe me, Stam, I would have never—I'd cut off my right hand before I'd—"

"I know, Jerry—I know," said Stam. "I just wondered, is all."

"Maybe I could embezzle some money from my dad's company," Jerry said.

"I wouldn't do that, Jerry," Stam said. "In the first place, you don't know anything at all about embezzling. You have to know what you're doing before you do something you're not supposed to do. In the second place, I don't want to be responsible for turning you to a life of crime."

Jerry would make a terrible criminal. He would lose his gun, and his getaway car couldn't start. And he would leave clues everywhere.

"There's just one thing to do," Stam said.

"What is it?" I asked him.

"Nothing," said Stam. "There's nothing to do since I don't have the money. I don't think anybody will actually kill me. Even if they killed me," Stam pointed out, "that would still leave you two guys. You two guys know too much. They would have to kill you too."

Jerry looked sick. "I wish your mother would let me move in here."

"It's probably better if we're not all under the same roof," Stam told him.

"But how about you and Chance?" Jerry wanted to know. "You and Chance are under the same roof."

"But we're different ages," Stam said, "and we move in different social strata."

As soon as Stam starts talking that way, he loses Jerry. Which is the general idea.

"I think I'll go home," Jerry said. "I want to lie down for a while."

"Now don't worry, Jerry," Stam told him. "If anybody gets you, Chance and I will know who did it."

"Oh, yeah," said Jerry, "sure."

"And vice versa," said Stam.

"And vice versa," said Jerry like a parrot and sort of stumbled out.

"Remember what you said about everything being so boring?" I said to Stam then.

He smiled and nodded.

"Well, it was really dumb," I said.

"I know," he said.

My mother came in then, staggering under the load of a big turkey and saying that next week was Thanksgiving and she was lucky she thought of it at all.

"Thanksgiving?" I said. "And this weekend is Homecoming and the dance. I have to call Tina and talk to her about the dance." That would be something nice to do, and I was glad I'd thought of it. After you think about something terrible for a while, it's a very good idea to find something good to think about.

Since it was a costume dance, I thought Tina and I should decide what to wear. It would be really dumb if she went as Little Miss Muffet, for instance, and I showed up as Frankenstein. When people are pretty serious about each other, they even wear sweaters alike sometimes. I liked the idea of Tina and me wearing things alike to show that we were serious.

Her voice when she answered sounded smaller than usual. "Hello," she said as if she didn't know who it was. As if she didn't know. "Chance? Oh, hi."

"What are you going to wear to the dance?" I asked her. "It's this weekend, you know, so I thought I'd better find out. Because I'd sort of like to be Dracula, but I thought that might not fit in with what you're planning to be. Do you know what you're going to be yet, Tina?"

"What I'm going to be?"

"Well, you know it is a costume dance," I said. "I thought if we had clothes sort of alike, it would be better. Like Romeo and Juliet, you know." I meant that I loved her like Romeo did Juliet. I wouldn't say that, but I meant that.

"Oh," she said.

"Romeo and Juliet might be kind of hard," I said. "How about Adam and Eve?" That was a terrible thing to say. Maybe she'd think I meant for her to go naked, for God's sake. "Or Mickey Mouse and Minnie?" I said. There, that was nice. Everybody knows Mickey and Minnie Mouse are very nice.

"I'm afraid I can't go to the dance with you, Chance," she said then.

I couldn't believe it. "Can't go to the dance?" I babbled. "With me?"

"Something's come up," Tina said. "I can't go to the dance with you after all, Chance. I'm sorry," she added.

"But of course you can go," I said. "You told me a long time ago that you would go. It's going to be a very special dance," I rattled on, "and you'll have quite a good time, Tina. I wanted you to go to this dance for a very special reason. There is a very good chance that you might get to be Queen, Tina," I said. I knew that I was acting really crazy but I was so shook, I couldn't help it. What did she mean, she couldn't go to the dance?

"Well, I am awfully sorry," she said, "but I really can't help it, Chance. Something has come up, and I can't go to the dance."

"But what is it?" I asked her. "What has come up? Why can't you go to the Homecoming Dance with me when you said you would? I've told everybody, all my friends. You've got to go to the dance with me, Tina."

"I should have told you before, Chance," she said. "There's somebody else."

"Somebody else?" My voice broke, and I didn't even care. "What do you mean, somebody else? Have you got another boy friend, Tina? Is that what you're trying to tell me? Is there some other guy you like better than me?"

"I'm really sorry, Chance," she said. "I didn't want to hurt you. I should have told you a long time ago, but I didn't want to hurt you."

"But you kissed me," I said. "The last time I saw you, you kissed me and I thought you meant it."

"Oh, kissing," she said. "What's kissing? Kissing isn't everything."

"But you could still go to the dance, couldn't you? Even if there is someone else, you could still go, couldn't you? You said you would, Tina. You definitely promised to go to the dance." I'd told everyone. I'd bragged about my girl. She couldn't do this to me.

"Well, I was going to," she said. "Believe me, I really meant to go to the dance with you, Chance. But the way it turned out, I think this other guy—I think he is going to take me out that night. It's very important because we have a lot of things to talk about. We might even get married."

"Married! So it must be someone older, huh?" I asked her.

"Yes, he's an older man. You know, Chance, that you're too young for me. I'm sorry," she said. "I didn't want to hurt your feelings."

"Maybe I was old enough when you didn't have anyone else," I said.

"Oh, Chance, please don't be mad. I think the world of you, I really do. You are a sweet boy, you really are, and I hope we can still be friends."

I saw red. I actually saw red—there were tears in my eyes like a red haze. "Friends?" I yelled at her over the phone. "Friends? Go to hell, Tina!" And I slammed the receiver down.

So now it was over. She had an older guy, and I had told her to go to hell. Now it was really over. But I had known for a long time, hadn't I? I had known, but I had hoped I was wrong. Another guy. An older guy who would touch Tina's breast and not stop there. Supposing I hadn't stopped that night? Would she still be my girl? Would she still be going to the dance with me? I thought that she would, and it made me very sad. Because that meant that nothing was the way I had thought it was, not love, not Tina herself.

"Dinner's ready," I heard my mother call from the kitchen, and I couldn't answer.

She came to the door then and called me again, "Chance, dinner's ready. Hurry up if you want to get anything."

"I'm sick to my stomach, Mom," I told her, and it was true. My stomach hurt and my head—and my heart. I could feel my heart actually aching.

She came in then and touched my forehead. "You don't feel feverish," she said. "Well, try to go to sleep and later, if you feel like it, you can have some tea and soup."

"I just want to go to sleep," I said.

Please leave me alone, Mom, I thought, before I cry.
I didn't want to cry, and I especially didn't want to cry
in front of my mom. Because she would hold me, she
would pat my head, and she would comfort me. I was
too old for that now. I was sorry, I didn't want to be
that old, I just was. All of a sudden, I was much older
than I had ever been.

I wanted to go to sleep, but how could I? Tina—the
Homecoming Dance where I might be King and she
would be Queen and not care that I was only fifteen
but almost sixteen. And I would never hold her again
or kiss her, and I had told her to go to hell. My girl was
gone; my brother was in danger. How could I go to
sleep? What was Stam going to do? Now he had no job.
He had no money, and Abe had threatened him on the
phone. I hated Tina, but I was afraid I couldn't stop
loving her. What was going to happen to me—to Stam?
How was it ever going to be all right?

I lay in my bed for a long time with my eyes closed
and when my mother came in later, I didn't answer her
and pretended that I was asleep. And pretty soon I was.

chapter 13

AT FIRST I THOUGHT I wouldn't go to the dance. To tell you the truth, I didn't really think I could. I thought it would just kill me to go to that dance without Tina. But then I knew that I had to. Because if I couldn't handle this, maybe I couldn't handle anything. Maybe when I grew up, if things got tough, I would just sit in a corner and play with my toes and drool or something. So I had to go.

I didn't have a date, and I didn't even try to get one. Because I didn't really expect to have a good time. It was just something I had to do. I had really spread it around what a great girl I had, so I wasn't looking forward to showing up without her. But if I didn't go at all, it would be worse. Because then everybody would say that I was really shot down, and there was no way I was going to let that happen. So I went to the dance, and I told everybody that Tina had the flu and I guessed that later I would tell them she had died.

When they announced who was going to be Home-coming King, I was leaning against the wall drinking a Coke and looking like I didn't give a damn. Which I didn't. Which it turned out lucky I didn't because Harley Whitcomb was voted King. A lot of people, mostly girls, came up to me and said it was just terrible I didn't win and that they had voted for me. The way I felt, I thought probably nobody had voted for me. And I didn't really care. I only cared about one thing—getting through the dance and staying cool. Which I did. Maybe it was because I was just numb, but I was probably the coolest guy there; and I could see that nobody was sorry for me about anything—not having my date or not getting to be King. Which was the way I wanted it and why I went to the damn dance in the first place.

I didn't even go home early, which I wanted to do. I never wanted to go home so much in my life as I did at that dance. For one thing, my face was aching. No lie—it was actually aching from having to look cool all the time. And even if I didn't care about the King stuff, I couldn't keep from thinking how Tina would have looked with that crown on her head, being Queen. And how she would have turned to me and smiled and squeezed my hand the way she did. I really tried not to think about things like that because it is hard to pre-tend that you don't care about anything when you re-member something you did care about.

I didn't go get pizza after the dance, though, with

the rest of the kids. "I have to call the hospital," I told them, "and see how Tina is."

"She's in the hospital?" asked this one girl named Jane something. "She must be pretty sick."

"She might die," I said.

I figured that in a few days I would say that she hadn't died but had gone to Arizona to get over the tuberculosis she got from the flu. It would be better than her dying, for me that is. Because if she died, everyone would expect me to really break up. I'd have to stay out of school for the funeral at least, and I knew my mother would take a dim view of that. Oh, she might let me if I explained the whole thing to her. But I didn't want to explain it to anyone. I never wanted to tell anyone the truth about Tina. It seemed like if nobody else knew the truth, I could sort of fix it up in my own mind eventually so it wouldn't be so bad. Maybe I would decide finally that I hadn't liked her so well after all. I hoped I could work something out so I wouldn't have to live the rest of my life in misery. I tried to think about the fact that Tina had a rather large nose, being Italian. But to tell the truth, she had a very beautiful nose. Just because she put me down didn't make her nose ugly. It would have been so much easier for me if it had. The terrible thing about me is that I can hardly ever fool myself even when I try. I just have to live with things the way they are. But I can usually do that. I've found out that I can. And that includes Tina.

But I couldn't go eat pizza because there was a lump in my stomach already from spending about four hours not having a good time and acting like I was. I thought that if I ate pizza, I might throw up. Of course I could always say I'd caught the flu from Tina. But I didn't want to throw up even if I did have an excuse for it. I hate throwing up. Like I've said before, I like to be in control of myself and when you're throwing up, you hardly ever are. So that's why I didn't go eat pizza.

John McKay and a few other guys walked home with me from the dance. We live only about two blocks from the high school. They wanted to come in and mess around for a while, but I said I had to call Tina.

"I don't want to talk to her with you guys here, for crissake," I said.

"How can you talk to her," Skeeters said, "if she's about dead? They don't let you talk to people in the hospital at midnight anyway. I know because my mom was in the hospital and they don't let them talk on the phone after nine o'clock at night. That's even when they're not dying. If they're dying, it's probably only about seven-thirty."

"They know it's the only thing keeping her alive," I said, "talking to me on the phone. Christ, they're not worrying about rules when it's a question of keeping her alive, are they?" I can really lie pretty well to other people. It's only myself I can't lie to.

So, anyhow, all those guys shoved off and I could finally go in the house and into my room and lie down on my bed in the dark. For a minute I was almost happy, it felt so good being all by myself in the dark and not having to pretend anymore. Then my mother stuck her head in the door and asked me if I had a good time and if I wanted something to eat.

"Or did you go for pizza?" she asked.

"I wasn't hungry." I tried to get the cool sound back in my voice. It was sort of hard after relaxing for a minute.

"Too bad about Tina," Mom said. "I hope she feels better soon."

I'd told Mom that too, about Tina having the flu. I didn't feel bad at all about lying to Mom about that. The older I get, the more I know you can't always tell your mother the truth. Which mothers spend their whole lives telling you that you must. Of course I don't lie to her except for her own good, so she won't worry. Or feel sorry for me, like about Tina. Because if Mom had known about Tina, she might have put her arms around me and patted my head and said something like, "There, there," the way you do with babies when they're crying. And you know, the dumb part is that I would have liked that in a way. But it would have made it harder. Honest to God, it's harder to get over things if your mother says, "There, there," to you, no matter how good it feels at the time.

So I just yawned and said to Mom, "Man, I'm just beat from all that dancing. Guess I'll go to sleep."

That always pleases her because I hardly ever go to

sleep deliberately and never as soon as she wants me to. I knew she would go out and leave me alone if I said I was going to sleep, which she did.

I wasn't planning to go to sleep though. What I was planning was something that I knew was stupid, but it was something I had to do. I was going to go to Tina's house and I was going to see the guy she'd turned me down for. Of course he might have already brought her home from their date, and how would I know? I mean how would I even know if she was there or if she was still out? See what I mean about how dumb it was? I couldn't knock on the door to find out if she was home. I couldn't do that. I didn't want her ever to know that I even cared. But I did care, and I had to try to find out. It was midnight now, and so I figured an older guy wouldn't have brought her home yet. Even a little fifteen-year-old like me had gotten to stay out till twelve. With an older guy, it would probably be later. I was going to try to see Tina's older boyfriend. I was going to watch him bring her home and kiss her goodnight, and then I was going to forget all about her. Sure I was.

I waited until the house was quiet. Mom and Dad were in their room; Stam was out somewhere. I put on my warmest clothes because it was a cold November night and I didn't want to get pneumonia just because I was crazy. Would Tina be sorry if I got pneumonia and died? Well, I knew *I* would be sorry if I did—to say nothing of my whole family.

When I went out of the house, I shut the front door very quietly so my mother wouldn't hear me. And then I waited on the front step for a moment in case she had. Because if she had, she would have come tearing right out demanding to know what in the world I was doing. When she didn't come, I took my bike from behind the bush where I'd parked it and wheeled it down to the corner. I didn't get on until I got to that corner. I'll tell you my mom has such a good ear she would have even heard me riding my bike down the drive.

It was cold. Even with my warm clothes on and a stocking cap and a scarf around my neck, it was cold. And I had a long ride to south Denver, but somehow it seemed right that I should be physically miserable since I was mentally miserable.

Long before I got there, though, I was sorry that I had started. My hands felt numb; I didn't think my nose would ever be the same again; and even under the cap and scarf, my ears seemed about ready to break off. But there was no use turning back now. There wouldn't be any point to all the suffering if I didn't go all the way now. I didn't even care about Tina anymore. All I cared about was getting home again and getting in my warm bed. What's a girl at the side of a couple of heavy blankets? That's how cold I was.

It seemed like hours before I wheeled into Tina's street, and I might have to stay out in the cold for another couple of hours before she came home. But I had to see this guy for myself. So I would have to wait no matter how cold I got.

But there was a car in front of Tina's house, and there were two people in the front seat. So I wouldn't have to wait. I wouldn't have to freeze to death because they wouldn't sit out in the car long on a night like this. And then I would ride down to Denny's on Broadway, which is open all night, and I would get some hot coffee and get warm before I started home. I was glad it was almost over.

I was at the corner when I saw the car and the two silhouettes in the front seat. I was a little closer when I knew the car. I stopped and leaned my bike against a tree halfway down the block. I didn't have to go any farther now that I knew. I couldn't go any farther. I didn't know how I would even ride home or even be able to keep living. Because it was Stam, you see. It was my brother Stam's car in front of Tina's house. Stam, my brother.

chapter 14

I HADN'T EXPECTED Stam to be home by the time I got there, but he was. It made me madder than ever to think of him riding home in a nice warm car while I froze.

What was I going to say to him? Stam and Tina. I was too shocked even to believe it. But I knew it was true. It explained a lot of things that I would understand as soon as I thought about it. For now, I had to get warm. I didn't want to talk to Stam tonight. The only thing I wanted to do was to get into bed where it would be warm.

It felt so good to be in bed with the blankets wrapped around me like a cocoon and the pillow over my head. It was so wonderful to be through with the terrible night—away from the dance where I'd had to act cool, away from the sight of Stam's car in front of Tina's house. I was almost happy snuggled there in my bed just because I wasn't cold anymore. I went easily to sleep in the warmness.

But in the morning as soon as I opened my eyes, I remembered. "We might get married," Tina had said. All the times she'd called in the last few weeks, it had been Stam she'd wanted to talk to instead of me, but she had been too chicken to tell me that. And Stam— the nights I'd thought he was with Cecelia, had he really been with Tina? Those nights when she'd told me not to come over because she had homework. Baby Chance. Fool Chance.

What was I going to say to him? What do you say to your brother when he does something like that to you? I got out of bed and went into his room. He was asleep of course. It was Sunday morning, and naturally he was asleep. Lying curled up on his side and smiling in his sleep as if he hadn't done anything to anybody, didn't know a bookie named Abe, hadn't lost his job.

"Wake up." I shook him. "Wake up, you sonofabitch."

He opened his eyes and grinned at me. Yawned and stretched his arms wide. "Hi, Chance," he said, "what's happening?"

"It isn't what's happening," I said. "It's what's already happened."

"The Mob?" he wanted to know. "So early in the morning?"

"How was your date last night?" I asked him.

He looked at me for a moment as if he wondered how much I knew. "It wasn't really a date," he said, "just some girl who's always bugging me."

"I know that girl," I said. "That was my girl."

"Stupid little bitch," he said. "I suppose she told you."

"She didn't tell me," I said. "And you didn't tell me. Why didn't you tell me, Stam?"

"I didn't know," he said. "You didn't say that she was your girl, Chance."

"But you knew! You must have known. I'm the one who met her. You knew how much I liked her, Stam. I loved Tina—I really loved her." I hadn't meant to say that. Whimpering like a baby.

"Well, I knew you were kind of hung up on her at first," he said, "but she was too old for you, kid. I thought you really knew she was too old."

"I'm almost sixteen."

"I'm not talking about years, Chance. That girl has a lot older ideas than you do."

I didn't say anything. I didn't want him to tell me what he meant by that.

"Remember that night she got so mad at you? The night I was supposed to pick you up at her house?" he said.

I remembered.

"She wanted you to screw her, that's why she was mad."

Tina? My sweet Tina? I'd apologized to her for touching her, had been ashamed of myself for touching her breast.

"And then when I came and there she was with no clothes on—" He shrugged his shoulders. "She asked for it." He got out of bed and reached for his jeans, and I hit him. Hit him in the mouth while he stooped for his jeans.

"You sonofabitch," I said.

Stam fell back onto the bed and there was blood on his mouth. He stared at me with the trickle of blood in the corner of his mouth. "I'm sorry, kid," he said. "You never told me. She's just a girl with hot pants. They're all over this town. You don't want to love her, a girl who will let anyone into her."

"Are you going to marry her?" I asked him, and my fist was still clenched.

"Marry her? Why the hell would I marry her? Just because I screwed her one time, more or less to be polite? I've been damn sorry I did too," he said, "the way she's bugged me since then. That's why I told her I would come over last night, to try to get her off my back." He touched his mouth and stared at the blood on his finger. "You've got a tough right there, kid," he said, trying to make a joke of it that I'd hit him, trying to make everything all right.

We had wrestled and boxed and given each other nosebleeds even if he was lots bigger than I was. We'd always done that, but we'd never hit each other on purpose before.

"How about taking a ride up to Morrison with me?" Stam asked me then. "Hamburgers and fries on me?"

As if I was a little kid, a little kid who could be comforted with a hamburger and some french fries. I didn't answer him; I turned away and went out of his room and into my own.

If I had done it to Tina that night, the way she wanted me to, she wouldn't have reached out for Stam, would she? She would have still been my girl, and we would have been real lovers. So I really was too young for her. I was only a little kid who didn't know anything about love after all. But wasn't it love when you wanted to be with a person all the time and liked to see her smile and just wanted to make her happy? Wasn't it love when you wanted to know things about her like her favorite color and what kind of games she liked when she was a little girl? Love was like that too, wasn't it, besides just wanting to screw a girl? The way it had been in the beginning was the way I would have liked to remember it. But Stam had even ruined my memories. If it hadn't been Stam, it would have been someone else. I knew that, but still I couldn't forgive him. Because he should have known. He was my brother; he should have known.

I heard Dad in the kitchen then, talking to Mom. "And of course I won't find out for sure," he said, "until the first of the year. But that's the word, and I think I can count on it."

"That's wonderful, Charlie," said Mom. "It's what you've always wanted, isn't it? It had to happen sometime because you really deserve it."

So what were they talking about? It sounded like something good. I was really in the mood to hear something good so I went into the kitchen. Stam was there, too. He and Dad were at the table drinking coffee, and Mom was at the stove frying eggs.

"Guess what, Chance?" my mother said to me when I came into the kitchen. "Dad's going to be a principal!"

"Boy, that's really great," I said and I sat down at the table. "I'm really glad to hear that, Dad."

He was smiling and looking pleased with himself. "Not too bad, huh? After all these years. I can hardly believe it, but this guy at the administration building told me, and I guess it's a sure thing. I won't know what school until the first of the year, but I'm going to be a principal at last."

"You'll have to have some new clothes, Charlie," Mom said. "Principals have to look nice."

Dad looked like he didn't know if he would like that part of it or not. "Why do I have to look so nice?" he asked. "It's what I do that will count, not what I wear. I think I can do a pretty good job. I have a lot of ideas for the job."

"What job?" It was Jerry strolling into the kitchen. He'd just wandered into the house without knocking, the way he always did. "Has Stam got a new job?" he wanted to know. "I thought you said you were out of a job now that you're through at Bowen's," he said to Stam.

"It's Dad," Stam said. "Dad's going to be a principal."

"Well, it's not official yet." Dad was still grinning. "But it's something I can pretty well count on."

"A principal! Gee, Charlie, that's swell," Jerry said. "Did I ever tell you I'd like to be a schoolteacher? If I can figure out how to do it—that's what I want to be, a teacher."

"I didn't know that, Jerry," Dad said. "It's not a bad job. I always liked it pretty well. Oh, you never get rich, but it's a job that's pretty interesting. But nowadays most people think of teachers as babysitters."

"Being a teacher is important," Jerry said.

"A person would like to think so," Dad said, "especially if he is a teacher. I don't know—the years come and go, you have so many kids and you wonder if any of the things you have said to them or taught them make any difference in the long run."

"My English prof at C.U. said the most valuable thing to me anyone has ever said," put in Stam. "He said, 'Be.'"

"Be?" asked Jerry. "Be what?"

"Be quiet, Jerry," Stam said.

"You could probably get on as a substitute next year," Dad said to Jerry, "until there are some vacancies again. There aren't any in Denver now."

"The thing is," said Jerry, "some of the courses I took

were the wrong ones, and I don't have my certificate." That figured—Jerry taking the wrong classes. If he was a teacher, he'd probably go to the wrong school. "Maybe I will take a couple of classes at night so I can get a certificate," Jerry said.

"Well," said Dad, "if you think you'd like being a teacher. I always liked it. Of course I've wanted to be a principal for a long time. More money for one thing. We can sure use more money—right, Lora?"

"It isn't the money," Mom said. "It's because you've wanted it for so long. It's what you've always wanted to do."

"I know," said Dad. "That's what I've always wanted."

"Can I have a couple of eggs, Lora?" asked Jerry. "I haven't had any breakfast, and I'm pretty hungry for some reason."

"You're always pretty hungry for some reason," Mom said, but she got two more eggs out of the refrigerator.

"And some coffee." Jerry jumped up from the table. "I'll get it myself." He reached for the coffeepot on the stove and hit Mom's elbow just as she was cracking the eggs into the skillet.

Mom stared down at the egg on her slipper. "I hate raw eggs on my feet," she said, "especially at dawn."

"It isn't dawn, Lora," Dad mentioned. "It's ten o'clock, that's hardly dawn."

"I don't even like eggs on my feet at ten o'clock," she said.

"I came over here to offer Stam a job," Jerry said, and it wasn't too dumb of him to change the subject like that.

"I really hate jobs," Stam said, "but I guess I have to have one."

"This is just till after Christmas," Jerry said. "It's for my folks, delivering stuff to some of those towns up in the mountains. You and I together—we'll take turns driving the truck. It's a pretty good way to get out of town," he mentioned, and I knew what he meant.

"Yeah."

Stam and I looked at each other and grinned. I didn't really mean to grin at him, but I'd been doing that my whole life, and it was sort of hard to get over.

"Maybe on the weekends Chance could go along and help us," Stam said.

"Sure he could," Jerry said. "Chance can go with us sometimes."

"If I want to," I said.

"We'll have a good time," Stam said.

I guessed we probably would.

chapter 15

I WAS OLDER NOW. Weeks went by, and it was December and not long until Christmas, and I was older. I wasn't mad at Stam anymore, and I was putting Tina out of my mind most of the time. But I wasn't the same anymore. I wasn't glad or sorry about it, that's just the way it was.

There was a girl in my algebra class I was always getting into arguments with, and I thought I'd ask her to the New Year's dance. Her name was Lynn Powers, and she was a very smart girl with a pretty big bust. Her eyes looked like she was about ready to laugh, and she was always putting me down. I figured she might be the one I was going to lose my virginity with, but I'd have to be careful. She was on the girls' gym team, and she might just break my arm or something.

Stam was still working for Jerry's folks, driving that truck up in the mountains. A couple of times I'd gone with them, and we'd had a lot of laughs and even got caught in a blizzard once, which was scary but very exciting. But most of the time I had to work at Sojo's. Seppi had gone to California, and I was the senior busboy there now. I didn't worry about giving Stam some of my money anymore. He didn't seem to worry about the money, so why should I? Of course I did, a little. I hadn't changed that much. But I was saving my money for Christmas, to buy everybody gifts.

We had already sent my sister, Del, a Christmas box to Rome since she couldn't come home. We made a tape to send her with all of us saying something and singing songs, which sounded pretty terrible since none of us can sing, but I knew Del would like it. I had a plan, one that I was going to start saving money for after Christmas. I was going to go to Rome myself as soon as I got out of high school. I would be old enough then so that my mother would let me go. I hadn't seen my sister for so long that I'd forgotten what she looked like. I was sorry that even when she was home, I'd never gotten to know Del that well. It had always been Stam. Stam had always been the most important one in the family to me. And maybe he still was, but there were other people there too. I was going to Rome to see my sister as soon as I could.

But now I was thinking about Christmas, smelling the sweet spiciness of cookies baking, hiding the presents I bought but never looking for the ones my mother hid. When I was a little kid, I did that. I always found all my presents before Christmas and knew what they were. But when you get older, you like surprises more because you don't have as many of them. I had bought everyone's gift but Stam's. I wanted to get him something special, something that would make things the same between us. Even while I was wondering what that could be, I knew there wasn't such a thing. Remember that poem about turning time back in its flight, make me a child again just for tonight? That's what I wanted, something like that. There wasn't anything like that, but I kept looking.

And all of a sudden it was two days before Christmas, and Mom and I were in the kitchen frosting Christmas cookies. I have always done this, putting the sprinkles on the Christmas trees, the cinnamon drops for buttons on the Santa Clauses. Every year I think that I am really too old, that this will be the last time I'll decorate the cookies. But every year I do it, partly because my mom likes me to, but mostly because I want to. Even when I am about sixty, I think I'll decorate Christmas cookies.

We were having cocoa while we did the cookies and talking the way we always do about lots of things and even telling some jokes. A time my mom and I always have together.

"Hey, Mom, how's your book coming?" I asked her.

She ruffled her hand through her hair in a way she has that makes it stand up all over her head. "Migawd," she said, "it's killing me! Backbreaking labor, nervous prostrations—I've never done anything so terrible!" She smiled then. "And I just love it. I think about it all the time, and the first draft is almost done."

"What's it about, Mom?" I asked her, and she rolled her eyes.

"It's about everything. Everything I know and have done. Love, hate, war—the universal experience. I may have to narrow it down."

"Focus," I said, "you're going to have to focus it somewhere." I can talk the lingo to my mother, and she really appreciates it. "How about your queries to publishers," I asked her; "get any leads?"

"All of them said they'd like to see it when it's done," she said.

"Great. If Dad is going to be a principal and you're going to sell a book, I guess we'll be rich."

"Being happy with what you do is a lot more important than being rich," she said.

It's a funny thing about her—she can say things like that with a straight face and it sounds logical because she believes it. I don't know if that is the truth or not, but my mom believes it.

We heard Dad come into the house then. We always know when it's Dad because he turns the television on as he goes through the living room. He came out into the kitchen carrying a pile of Christmas presents. "I told them all not to give me presents," he said, "but most of them did anyway."

Every year the kids in my dad's room at school load

him down with gifts, mostly after-shave lotion with names like "Sexee" and "Devilish."

"Are you going to open them now or on Christmas?" I asked him.

"Oh, I wouldn't open my presents before Christmas," he said like he was shocked at the idea. He's just like a little kid sometimes—it's kind of nice, it really is.

"I was just telling Chance," my mother said to Dad then, "that liking your job is more important than being rich."

Dad put down the packages, took off his coat and hung it on the back of a chair. "You always know it all, Lora, don't you?" he said to her, but he was smiling. He sat down at the table and Mom got him a cup of cocoa. He was still smiling and shaking his head. "I swear, Lora," he said, "I don't know how you do it. It's as if you read my mind. It's scary, that's what it is. Why can't I have any secrets from you?" And he reached across the table to pat her hand.

"After twenty-two years, Charlie Hamilton," Mom said, "I ought to know you."

What were they talking about? It had something to do with love and being married a long time, I guessed. But what did it mean?

"I thought I wanted to be a principal," Dad said. "Up until today, I was sure I wanted to be a principal. And then all the presents, and little Jimmy Malone made me a card and put a nickel in it. You know how poor the Malones are," he said to Mom, "a nickel means a lot to Jimmy. And I knew I wasn't going to see any of them anymore, knew I was going to be stuck in an office and not see any kids anymore unless they misbehaved. What kind of a way is that to see kids, just when they're naughty?"

"You're a good teacher, Charlie," Mom said. "Any able administrator can be a good principal. It takes love to be a good teacher, Charlie."

"And you knew." He shook his head again like he couldn't believe it.

My mother and father really loved each other, that's what it all meant. You don't have to be a principal or sell a book or even be rich if someone loves you and you love her. That's what it meant. I hoped that it was true.

"When's Grandmother Hamilton coming?" Mom asked Dad then.

"Tomorrow afternoon at five o'clock," Dad said. "Christmas Eve."

"And then the whole family for dinner on Christmas Day," Mom said as if she was going to have a good time instead of cook all day. "Did I tell you Poppy is bringing his new girlfriend? She is thirty-five, and Poppy says they are going to get married. Can you imagine? Marrying a young woman like that—why, it will kill Poppy."

"But what a way to go," said Dad.

chapter 16

IT WAS THE DAY before Christmas, Christmas Eve, and I still hadn't bought Stam's present. So I got up that morning and rode my bike to the shopping center. I wanted to get just the right thing, and I hadn't found it yet. I sort of thought about a Shakespeare book with a leather cover and golden letters on it, but I didn't have enough money. I didn't want to just get him a shirt or a tie. For one thing, I didn't think he would ever wear a tie again in his life if he could possibly help it, and shirts don't mean that much to him either.

I finally got the perfect thing—a world marble. Have you ever seen one of those? It's about the size of a little kid's bouncing ball and made out of blue plastic. As you turn it around, you see different things—mountains and flowers and trees and snow and sunsets. No lie— you can see all those things and more when you turn that world marble. I thought Stam would like it more than anything he ever had.

It was almost noon when I got home and Mom was out in the kitchen cutting up vegetables for the Christmas Eve stew. She was already cooking the meat, and it smelled great.

"Did you know that your brother is crazy?" is what Mom said to me when I came out to show her the world marble.

I didn't really want to hear about how crazy Stam was when I had just spent $7.95 on him, but I knew I was going to hear it anyway.

"He moved," she said. "Moved on the day before Christmas."

"Moved? Where? Why?"

"Jerry came by with his truck and they loaded it up and took off," Mom said. "Where, I don't know. Why, I don't know. Except Stam is Stam and always does things like that."

Had the bookie found Stam? Was that why he had moved so fast, getting out of the house on the day before Christmas, because the bookie had found him?

"Was he—nervous?" I asked Mom. "I mean, did he act worried about anything?"

She looked at me and raised her eyebrows. "Nervous? Stam? He was singing carols and beating on his snare drum the last I saw of him going down the walk. Now —Jerry," she said. "Jerry was nervous. He set a bottle of beer in the mailbox and it spilled and I don't know what the mailman is going to think."

Yeah, Jerry would have been nervous if the bookie

had found Stam. And Stam would have been beating a drum and singing. It figured—geez, it all really figured.

"Listen, Mom, you haven't seen a really tough-looking guy hanging around here, have you?"

"If you mean Santa," Mom said. "He won't come until you're asleep tonight. A really tough-looking guy? What exactly are you talking about, Chance? Is somebody after Stam? Some girl's husband or something?"

Her eyes were getting big now, and I said quickly, "Nobody's husband is after Stam, Mom. It's nothing, really nothing. I just thought it was funny, him moving on Christmas Eve."

"If it were anybody but Stam, it would be funny," Mom said. "For Stam, that is normal behavior. Actually, it is not that funny. Actually, it is sickening."

It was sickening all right. After thinking it over, I didn't think the bookie had found Stam at all. If a bookie did find him on the day before Christmas, Stam would just say he had to make popcorn balls and hang his stocking and how about checking back in a couple of days. He really would.

But why had he done that—moved on Christmas Eve? I thought maybe he'd gone too far this time. I wasn't going to think it was funny this time no matter what he'd done—rented a casket, built an igloo. I wasn't going to go along with it this time. Because it was Christmas.

Grandmother Hamilton was coming this evening, and

I was going to sleep in Stam's room tonight. Put my sleeping bag down on his floor, talk late, have something to eat. It was going to be so nice, Stam and I talking in the dark with the snow coming down outside the windows and the moon making the ice glitter on the windows. Because it was snowing already. It was going to be snowing tonight, snowing on Christmas Eve with the house smelling good and knowing that tomorrow was the Christmas tree.

I was practically grown up, being fifteen and almost sixteen. But nobody wants to be grown up on Christmas. It is the only time of year when I really want to feel like a little kid. How could he do this to me on Christmas? How could he? I felt like I'd found out there wasn't any Santa Claus, which I'd known for a long time—since I was about five, I guess. But it was the first time I'd ever felt bad about it. No Santa Claus—no Stam.

But of course the bookie could have found him. Maybe even Stam would run if a bookie found him. I didn't think he would though.

"But will he be back?" I said to Mom. "Will he be back for tonight? It's going to be Christmas Eve."

"It's always been you two, hasn't it?" she said. "The rest of us here and part of it all, but it's always been you two—you and Stam. He has to go away sometime. Don't you know that? Poor little Chance—don't you know that?"

I just hated her calling me "Poor little Chance" and saying that Stam had to go away. "Why does he?" I said. "Why the hell does he?"

She stood behind my chair at the kitchen table and put her arms around my shoulders. It didn't feel too bad, her arms around me. It felt good actually. "You'll go too," she said. "All of you have to go. Nothing stays the same. There's a lot out there, Chance. There's something out there for each one of you."

It's kind of embarrassing when she talks that way, and yet, I like it too. It makes me think that life is big and wonderful and scary. It makes me proud to be part of it and lonely too in a funny way. Lonely for all the people you see maybe one time and then never see again. Somebody on a street corner who smiles at you when you go running by to catch a bus. Maybe it would be somebody you'd really like if you got to know him. I don't always know exactly what my mom means by what she says, but the neat part of it is that there are all kinds of things she could mean. All kinds of things you think of when she talks that way. We weren't all going to be together forever; she meant that, I knew. But I wanted us to be together for a while yet—I wanted us to be together for Christmas.

"Well, Stam ought to be home for tonight," I said. "It's Christmas Eve, for crissake." And then I was ashamed of myself for swearing like that on Christ's birthday.

"I'm not saying yea or nay," Mom said, "because I don't know. I have no idea what anyone is going to do except for me, and I'm not even positive about me."

But I thought Stam would come home any minute, probably bringing Jerry for supper. Busting in with some crazy story, but home for Christmas Eve. I didn't really worry about it that much, because I was sure he would.

Grandmother Hamilton came at five, and it was dark by then and we had the Christmas tree lights on. We didn't eat until almost six-thirty because Mom was waiting for Stam too. She didn't say that she was, but I knew she was.

"Well, where's Stam?" Grandmother asked finally. "Working late at his job?" she said, like she hoped that was it. "He'd get overtime on Christmas Eve, wouldn't he?" Grandmother loves for people to work and get overtime.

"I don't know exactly where Stam is," Mom said, like it didn't matter at all. "He's the funniest boy," she said. But she wasn't laughing.

So all of us ate stew and biscuits without Stam. I had been smelling that stew all day and thinking how good it was going to taste, but I couldn't eat much for some reason. Well, actually it was because of Stam— because I felt so bad about Stam. I had been sure all afternoon that he would come home; but as soon as it got dark, I wasn't sure anymore. In fact, I was sure he wouldn't. It's a lot harder to hope for something at the end of the day than it is at the beginning, or even in the middle. Have you ever noticed?

"He'll be here pretty soon," Dad said. "Can you imagine Stam passing up Christmas Eve stew?"

"Stam moved," I said, because I figured they might as well know it and face it. I might as well face it.

"Moved?" asked Dad like he couldn't believe it.

"On Christmas Eve?" That was Grandmother Hamilton. "The boy must have taken leave of his senses."

"Well, I don't know," said Mom. "I don't actually know. But he moved his bed and his drums. Jerry had his truck, and he and Stam loaded the stuff in."

"But what did he say?" asked Dad. "Didn't he say where he was going?"

"He said he had found his place," said Mom. "He said, 'See you later.' I was going to ask him more—I was going to ask him a lot—but I was afraid Jerry would drop the bed on me if I got too close. And then they were gone. Just like that—gone."

So that was it. Stam had found his place, and it wasn't like I thought it would be at all. I had thought he would talk to me about it. I had sort of thought he would take me to his place with him. I never thought he would go off without even saying goodbye.

"I'll have some more stew," I said. I'd just be damned if I was going to waste away and not eat and get skinny because of my stupid brother. "If Stam's not coming, we can eat his share," I said.

"Shame on you, boy," Grandmother Hamilton said, "eating your brother's share."

"It's Jesus's birthday, remember," I told her, "not Stam's." He wasn't God Almighty, he really wasn't. What if I had spent fifteen years thinking so. He sure as hell wasn't.

My mom looked at me and smiled in that secret way she has that means I'm not fooling her. She always knows how I feel. She put another helping of stew on my plate. "I might save a little for Stam," she said, "just in case. You never know with Stam."

I knew what she meant. Wait and see, she meant. Maybe it's all right—maybe everything will be all right.

After supper, Grandmother and I did the dishes so that Mom could finish wrapping presents and Dad could watch a Christmas cartoon show on television. Can you believe it? No wonder all the kids in his school love him—he's one of them. I don't mean he is dumb, because my dad is actually very smart and can figure out any math problem. It's just that he's young in heart. It's really nice, isn't it? Sometimes I feel like I'm about forty years older than he is.

It took quite a long time to get the dishes done. I think Grandmother feels that the only time the dishes are really clean at our house is when she does them. "My stars," she says as she scrapes and scratches, "a body wouldn't believe it."

I tried to have a good time doing the dishes with her. I wrapped my tea towel around my back end and did a dance, although Grandmother took a dim view of that.

"You're getting germs on that towel, Chance," she said. "Stop that foolishness, boy."

"Grandmother, I haven't got a dirty little rumpus," I said. "I got me a clean little rumpus."

"Such talk," she said. "Lean over here, and I'll wash your mouth out with soap." But she was about to laugh. Grandmother's not a complete loss, she really isn't.

So we were having a good time on Christmas Eve, dancing and wrapping and watching TV, right? And if one person didn't want to come, well—it's a free country.

After the dishes, we played Monopoly and had Christmas cookies and hot chocolate. I always win at Monopoly, but this time I had it tough trying to beat Grandmother. Mom never wants to spend any of her money so she doesn't have much chance. Dad keeps leaving the table to call someone on the phone or check the ball scores on the radio so he doesn't actually participate that much. But Grandmother is like somebody on Wall Street—she'll screw anybody out of his last cent if she can do it. So it's not bad at all, playing Monopoly with her, and I almost forgot about Stam for a while. I was just determined to beat the pants off this old lady even if she was my grandmother. But finally she landed on my Boardwalk with a hotel on it and was going to have to mortgage almost everything.

"I can still make it back," she said, "you'll see. The old gray mare's got a couple of kicks left in her yet."

But it was midnight, and Mom said we really should go to bed. "We'll want to be up early to have the tree," she said, "and there'll be lots to do with everyone coming for dinner in the afternoon."

"Next time I'll nail you to the wall, boy," Grandmother said to me.

And I knew she would try. But I wouldn't let her if I could help it. Because it is really insulting to let people beat you at things. Insulting to them, I mean. And Grandmother is too sharp—she'd know if I let her beat me. So I never would. Besides, I am going to try my best to win at everything I do. Who knows what will happen to me when I grow up or what I'll be? I don't think I will be a ballet dancer or play the harpsichord; but otherwise, it's an open draft. One thing I don't mean to be, if I can help it, is a good loser. I mean to be a good winner.

Finally everybody was in bed; the lights were out, and it was time to go to sleep. "It's time now," I told myself. "Go to sleep," I told myself. But I didn't pay any attention. Finally I got up and went into the living room and plugged the Christmas tree lights in. Stam still might come, and it seemed like it would be terrible for him to come home to a pitch-dark house on Christmas Eve. I wasn't even sure Mom had saved him any of the stew.

I stood there and watched the little lights wink on and off for a while, and I wasn't mad at Stam anymore.

I tried to reach for it, but it wasn't there. And it was terrible for me, not being mad anymore, because now I was only sad. And that is much worse.

I lay down on the couch because I didn't want to go back in Stam's room. It didn't even look like his room anymore with his bed and drums gone. Of course there were still a lot of things on the floor, but for some reason it didn't look like his stuff anymore. Just some junk that didn't belong to anybody. Some junk that nobody wanted. I had put my sleeping bag down in Stam's room and tried to go to sleep, but it was too empty in there. Even with me in it, that room was too empty.

The couch wasn't any better. I couldn't go to sleep on the couch either. Even with my eyes shut, I could feel the Christmas tree lights blinking, and finally I got up and unplugged them again. Because it was dumb having them on, just wasting electricity having them on. A bunch of colored lights wasn't magic, for crissake. Some colored lights weren't going to bring Stam home.

What was I going to do without him? How was I going to get along without my brother? We had talked about Stam's place, but somehow I had never thought he would go there without me. In some crazy way, I had thought it would be my place too.

It must have been about four when Stam woke me up. Opening the front door and coming into the house and waking me up. Shaking me there on the couch and whispering, "Chance, come on. Wake up, Chance."

So it was all right, wasn't it? All right, but still not the same. It wasn't Christmas Eve anymore—it was Christmas morning. Time won't stand and wait.

"Merry Christmas, Chance," Stam said.

"Yeah, Merry Christmas."

"Get your clothes on," he said, "and come with me. I want to show you something."

"Your place, huh?" I said, like somebody who wants to spoil the punchline of a joke.

"My place," he said. "I found it, Chance."

I wanted to ask him why he hadn't come for Christmas Eve, for the stew and biscuits, for the family stuff on Christmas Eve. But he hadn't. So what was the difference why he hadn't?

"I don't know, Stam," I said, "it's pretty late. It's probably almost time for the Christmas tree. Maybe some other time. I'll be over to see your place one of these days." He hadn't said a word to me about it. He'd just found his place and gone off without saying anything to me. Christmas Eve was over now.

"We'll be back," he said. "We'll be back in plenty of time. I want you to have some Christmas at my house, Chance. I have a tree. And I have your present there."

"Well, okay," I said, "for a little while, I guess."

Because of course I knew I would go. Some things don't change. I probably would always do what Stam wanted me to do. But maybe now I would think about it first. Maybe I would decide whether or not I was going to do it.

I got my clothes from Stam's room and my present for him from under the tree, and we went out. The sky was very dark with clusters of stars and snow falling softly. Not too cold, but you could see your breath before you. Stam and I both stuck out our tongues to taste the snowflakes the way we always did as we went down the walk to his car.

"Is your place very far, Stam?" I asked him when we were in the car and driving down the street.

"That's one of the nice things about it," he said, "it's close to home. Later I will have a farther place; but to start with, it has to be near."

I knew what he meant. He was going away, but he was going slowly. When it was time for me to go, I meant to go fast and all at once, like a rocket.

We went about seven blocks, crossed Wadsworth Boulevard, down one street, and turned to the right.

"Here it is," said Stam, as he pulled off the street and into a field. "Here's my place, Chance. Day before yesterday, that's when I found it. Driving along the street and wondering what I was ever going to do and where I was ever going to go, and there it was. It was kind of Fate, you know—seeing it like that. And then of course I had to find out who owned it and if I could rent it. I wanted to get it all ready before I showed it to anyone. Of course Jerry had to know since I needed his truck, but Jerry doesn't care. He just moves things

and carries things, and he doesn't care. I think I will
stay here for a long time," said Stam. "Now that I have
found such a good place, I am going to stay in it."

"But it's a vacant lot," I said. "It's only a vacant lot."

What kind of crazy deal was this? Even Stam
wouldn't just live out in the middle of a vacant lot in
the winter, would he? I looked around for a tent, because it would be just like him—it really would. And
then I saw the shack. Behind some high weeds at the
back of the lot, away from the street and almost hidden
by the tall weeds and a couple of trees, there was a
shack. With a light in the window and a plume of smoke
coming out of the chimney. As we came nearer, I could
see that there was a falling-down fence around it with
a gate that hung crooked. But you could fix the fence,
I thought, and get a new hinge for the gate. It was only
a small place, a small wooden house that wasn't any
particular color anymore. There were high weeds on
each side of the front door, and Stam had hung Christmas ornaments on them that swayed and glittered in
the night.

"See?" he said. "I was getting everything ready for
Christmas. Isn't it lucky these bushes were here by the
front door? I can hardly wait for summer when everything grows."

I didn't tell him that they weren't bushes, only
weeds. And that it is really crazy to hang Christmas
balls on weeds. But they did look pretty hanging there,
turning slowly in the night air. If it was my place, I

would cut down the weeds and plant grass in the spring. I would fix the fence and paint the house.

Stam unlocked the door, and we went in. A one-room house, that's all it was, with Stam's bed in one corner, his drums in the middle of the floor, and a big black stove that glowed red with the fire inside. A kind of bathroom too, with a toilet and a shower, but no door. No door on the bathroom!

"A wood-burning stove," Stam said. "Isn't that lucky? I'll be warm here all winter, and it makes it cozy."

There was a Christmas tree too, just as Stam had said there would be. Little and scroungy and leaning crooked—he probably bought it because it was the worst-looking one and he felt sorry for it. No lie—that's the crazy way he is, twenty-one years old and feeling sorry for Christmas trees. Not people, only Christmas trees, things like that. But there were lights on it and a few ornaments and a star on top. There was one present underneath, and I knew it was mine.

"We're going to have champagne," he said, "with our Christmas tree." He opened the door and reached out in the snow to bring in the bottle. "Iced to perfection."

We had to drink out of the bottle because he didn't have any glasses yet. "I have lots of things to buy as soon as I make enough money," he said. "A table probably. I would like to have a table and maybe a couple of chairs."

"A door for the bathroom," I mentioned. "You could sure use a door for your bathroom."

He looked surprised as if he hadn't even noticed that. "Oh, yeah, a door. I'll make a list," he said, "of things I really need for my house."

"But you won't have a job, will you, after the first of the year?" I asked him. "I thought your job with Jerry's folks would be over after the first."

"I have a new job," he said, and he smiled. "A really great job. I worked tonight, and I'll work tomorrow night too." So Grandmother Hamilton had been right —Stam had been working at his job, whatever it was.

"I'm a cab driver," he said. "Isn't that wonderful? The best job I could get, and I never even thought of it. There was an ad in the paper this morning, and I went down and got hired. I can work whenever I want and not work if I don't want to. I lease the cab, you see, whenever I drive, so I am my own boss. I am going to take a geology class at C.U. Denver Center next semester and maybe botany in the summer."

"A cab driver?" I said. A cab driver. But he had a college degree. He was going to be a professor or something great. I had been waiting. Mom had been waiting. "I guess you're going to be a geologist," I said. "I think that will be neat, Stam, being a geologist." Babbling away. "Or a botanist. You said botany, didn't you? Maybe you're going to be a botanist."

"Don't you see, Chance?" he said. "That's the really great part of it. I don't have to be anything—I already am. I've been worrying about what I was going to be, and I never stopped to think that I am. Just me—I live, I am. I can read what I want and plant flowers here and study something just because I want to find out about it. I can drive a cab to make the money I need. And I'll see people, all kinds of people in the cab, people I'll want to know. And someday go to New Orleans or Frisco— anywhere. They have cabs almost everywhere you know. And play my drums and have a dog or cat. Everything, Chance," he said. "Isn't it great? I found my place just the way you said I would."

"But how about the money, Stam?" I asked him. "How about the thousand dollars you owe that bookie?"

"No problem." He smiled. "Everything's cool."

Cool? No problem? But I had been so worried. When Stam moved out, I thought the bookie had found him.

"What are you talking about?" I asked Stam. "You still owe that guy, don't you? He's still after you, isn't he?"

"No, and no," he said, and he smiled again. I wished he'd quit that smiling. When you've worried about something for months, laid awake at night and worried, you don't like somebody smiling about it and saying things like "Cool" and "No problem."

"So what happened? Tell me what happened," I said.

"I just went over to Baby's and saw Abe, and everything's fixed up," he said.

"But how?" I asked him. "How did you fix up a thousand dollar debt? And why didn't you tell me?"

It seemed like it was all I had thought about for so long.

"I don't know." Stam looked surprised. "I forgot, I guess. It wasn't that big a deal."

It had been a big enough deal to touch everything I'd done since summer and spoil it a little. Even when I'd loved Tina, even when I'd been happy, the worry over Stam had been there all the time.

"But how about the money?" I asked. "Isn't Abe going to make you pay the money?"

"Oh, I paid him," Stam said. "I gave Abe a thousand dollars."

"How?" I asked. "Where did you get it?"

"Well, actually it was Jerry who gave it to him," Stam said.

"Jerry paid Abe?" I couldn't believe it.

"Yeah, he went over to Baby's with me, and he paid Abe. It was Jerry's idea—"

"But how can you pay Jerry back?" Poor old Jerry, I thought.

"Oh, I'll pay him back eventually. No problem about that. It was his idea. He borrowed the money from his dad, I think. Old Jer's been really uptight about this whole thing. He really thought somebody was going to kill me." Stam laughed.

I knew the feeling. "Well, didn't you think so too?"

"Not really." He considered it. "Oh, at first I'll admit it entered my mind. But after a while, I didn't really think about it that much. Jerry never forgot about it though. Then last week somebody from Baby's got

Jerry's number from somewhere and called him. Scared the hell out of him."

Yeah, Jerry would have been scared all right. But he'd gone to Baby's with Stam anyway—gotten the money for Stam and gone with him. Scared shitless, but with Stam all the way.

Everybody loved Stam. And Stam? Who did Stam love? Who did Stam love as much as himself? Was there anyone at all Stam loved that much? I had thought it was me. It was something I'd always counted on.

"No problem," he'd said about the money. "I guess I forgot to tell you, not that big a deal," he'd said.

And now? And now. Stam and Chance—Chance and Stam—one in my mind, but two after all.

I would paint the shack and fix the fence. I would cut down the weeds. Was this Stam's place or only one of all the places? Would he always seek and find and seek again? Tina, the thousand dollars, the blood on his mouth where I'd hit him. Not a sonofabitch but just Stam. Stam, the way he'd always been, the way he'd always be. His place, my place. My brother—Stam—always my brother.

He lifted the champagne bottle and drank out of it and passed it to me. "Here's to you," he said.

I took the bottle and drank. "Mud in your eye, buddy," I said.

This is a first novel for Pat Lawler, whose short stories have appeared in numerous magazines for teenagers and adults including *McCalls, True Story, Ingenue, Datebook* and *Teen*. Sometime actress and luncheon speaker, Pat Lawler was born in an Oklahoma oil town and now lives in Colorado.